Praise for *ILLUS*

"*Illusion of an Ending* is a wonderful story of our closest relationships with their ups and downs. It is a tale of love and loss and of connecting with loved ones in the here and hereafter…Through the characters' actions and interactions with each other, Danielle gently and accurately weaves the metaphysical concepts of life beyond physical death, our continued connection with loved ones on the Other Side, the Akashic Records, and embracing our life paths into the story. Whether you are already well-versed in these topics or are just curious, this novel and its pearls of wisdom will appeal to you. I thoroughly enjoyed this book. "

–Val Silver, holistic healer and Award-winning author of *Rescue Me*

"A must-read for anyone interested in discovering the compelling and mysterious regions that silently wait for us outside of our daily comfort zones. Danielle does an excellent job of taking us through the dark as she whispers the strange secrets of life's synchronicities and invites us to explore the borders between inner and outer worlds."

–Natasha Ganes, Writer and Cofounder of *TreeHouseArts.me*

"A beautiful story by a talented writer demonstrating the magic and vastness of life and beyond."

–Sheri Fink, #1 Bestselling Author and President of The Whimsical World of Sheri Fink

ILLUSION

of an

ENDING

DANIELLE SOUCY MILLS

Illusion of an Ending
Copyright © 2014 by Danielle Soucy Mills

Aerial Awareness Media
PO Box 502563
San Diego, CA 92150

www.daniellesoucymills.com

Publisher's Note: *Illusion of an Ending* is a work of fiction. Names, characters, businesses, places, events, and incidents are either the products of the author's imagination or used in a fictitious manner. Any resemblance to actual events, companies, locales, or persons, living or dead, is purely coincidental.

Edited by Michelle Josette (www.mjbookeditor.com)
Cover photo by Elizabeth Gryzbinski
Cover design by Regina Wamba of MaeIdesign.com
Author photo by Chris Wood of SDPhotoStudio.com
Formatting and interior design by JT Formatting

Illusion of an Ending / Danielle Soucy Mills – 1st ed.
ISBN-13: 978-0991533848 | ISBN-10: 0991533844

For my grandmothers,
who continue to guide, help, and love,
especially from Beyond. Thank you.

And for my grandfathers,
who I don't remember meeting in this life
but I'm sure are very proud, just the same.
– D.S.M.

PROLOGUE

"Unable are the Loved to die
For Love is Immortality,"
– Emily Dickinson

Jimmy Pollaski

E very day of my life I died a new death.
As the years turned me from child to teenager to
adult, I remember wondering what it would feel like
to die. How would I know when it happened?

Now, as I ascend over my body lying lifeless in the hospital bed, I see everything at once, know everything at the same
time. My mother stands over me, her head low. She's waiting
for a sign to assure her that I'll be okay. My father sits behind
her. His mind is racing, face blank. He never knows the right
way to calm her down. Outside, the San Diego sun warms the
day to a pleasant seventy-four degrees.

I feel nothing but a rush of energy as the light around me grows brighter. Life isn't flashing before my eyes, like they say, but showing up in pieces that remind me things will not carry on as they were. I begin to recall events throughout my lifetime where I believed I was coming so close...to a close.

I thought once that dying would be like breaking my elbow after my bicycle flew out from under my eight-year-old body. Pain shot up my arm, folded under at an unnatural angle. Still alive years later, I swore that death would be like the feeling of my lungs collapsing as my track coach yelled, "Only ten more miles!" I thought death loomed after a fifteen-minute swim in November's North Atlantic, purple shaking lips and rubber skin. When that wasn't death, I was sure it would arrive the morning after kicking kegs in the woods as the night transformed into dawn.

I recognize my mother's worry that if the beer didn't kill us, maybe it would have been the eighty-foot jumps into the quarry's cavernous waters. The lofty shadows of trees drifted over our drunken heads, stars blinking through the branches. Our bodies floated in the cool water. Our sobriety was the only casualty then. The intoxication never shut me down completely, not even when my eyes shook to a close, opening again four hours later to the sun pouring rays at me as generously as I had let the alcohol flow down my throat. Head pounding, thinking in broken thoughts. Yes, finally, this had to be it. Really dying.

Now I know that these times were only attempts at escape, the way my mother closes her eyes but the world remains around her, the way people are unable to fully detach from the hurt and vulnerability which tie us hand-in-hand to life. We persevere, countless moments of pain leading us to this final moment of release.

Twenty-five years gone by, but it's my time.

"Mom, I'm okay! I'm right here!" My voice stifles as if I'm talking into layers of sheets that I can't lift.

My mother's chin rises. She pulls her cell phone from her pocket.

Thousands of miles away, my sister looks out her window at the snow-covered scenery. The streets are caked in thick ice. She's clutching the phone to her face, her eyes red and puffy as she dabs them with tissue.

The hospital staff urged my friends to go and rest hours ago. I see them asleep on the couches, the silent glow of the television lighting up the living room.

"I know you can't hear me now, but I will find a way. There is a way," I tell them.

It's only a matter of time before the days align. My path has led me here, the wind pressing against my face, the motorcycle's engine roaring beneath me. The earth and the ocean smear together at seventy miles per hour. Paths of everyone on Earth diverging, and intersecting.

I watch my mother collapse into the chair beside my dad, his arm cradling her descent. The doctor stands above them. All at once, I feel the delicate hand of my grandmother, its warmth transferring through my body like a comet grazing the sky with a sudden, hot glow. She's been waiting for me.

My mother's face contorts. She tosses her face into her hands, head shaking back and forth.

"My story isn't over, Mom," I say. "The beginnings and the endings aren't real. I promise, I will tell you the true story—our story."

As I speak, the scene closes in around me, forming a tunnel of astounding radiance. Shards of illumination multiply without hurting my eyes.

Today I am dying, yet I feel more alive now than ever before as the world around me fades to light.

CHAPTER
ONE

Patricia Pollaski

Tuesday -- February 3rd -- 10:17 a.m.

P atricia's ears rang with the beeping of the monitor. As she reached over, her arm brushed against the cords attached to the piece covering her son's mouth. She touched the top of her hand to his cheek. His skin felt warm and clammy. His chest moved up and down in a steady motion as if he were sleeping.

Patricia breathed in a stream of air through her nose, releasing it through her mouth. The hospital smelled like curdled milk. It was a similar stench to the nursing home where she worked, relentless and overbearing. The rooms, like the ones at Kendall Retirement, resembled nicely decorated jail cells. The bed sat at one side of the room, and a few chairs lined the wall at the other end just below the window.

"Why don't you sit, Patricia? You've been standing all

1

morning. Rest your feet a while," her husband said from one of the brown chairs behind her.

"I don't mind it," she answered. "Besides, I sat for way too long on that plane."

"That was hours ago."

"I'm okay." Patricia shut her eyes, the most recent events passing through her mind: the phone call relaying Jimmy's motorcycle accident, the red-eye flight to San Diego booked last minute, the arrival at Sharp Memorial Hospital just after the sun had risen over the California hills.

Patricia's cell phone buzzed in her pocket. She perked up at the sight of her daughter's number.

"Hi, honey."

"Hi, Mom," Denise said. "How's he doing?" Her daughter's voice resembled her son's.

Patricia sighed. "We're not sure yet. Still waiting on the doctor. You know how these medical personnel can be, always running around."

"Yeah, listen. The snow started falling here nonstop, and they shut down Logan Airport. I don't know if I'll make it out today," Denise said, her words filtered through sobs. "I'll try to get there as soon as I can. Please tell Jimmy that I love him."

"It's okay, Denise. I'll tell him. I'll give you a call once we get word from the doctor."

"Thanks, Mom. I'll talk to you soon." With a click, her daughter was gone.

Patricia backed away from the bed, collapsing into the seat beside her husband. Her son's last words ricocheted in her head. *I'll talk to you soon, Mom.*

"I should've called him the other morning when I said I would," Patricia said. "Then he would've been lying around in

2

bed like he always does on Monday mornings before class. He wouldn't have been leaving for school, in the way of that damn truck driver who didn't even have a license to drive that big thing."

Her husband rubbed her shoulder as she sunk into the chair. "You can't blame yourself," he said.

"I'm not, but...I can't help but wonder how things would've been if he hadn't moved to California. If we'd convinced him to stay at home in Gloucester like he planned."

"He's a grown boy, Patricia. He made his own decision to move. Things happen. We just have to stay strong."

Just then, the door clicked and opened.

Patricia set her shoulders straight. She faced the doctor who fiddled with the machine before surrendering his attention to her and the clipboard he held in one hand.

"So, what's the word?" she asked.

The doctor cleared his throat. "Well, Mr., Mrs. Pollaski," he said, looking at them in turn. "We've been monitoring the electrical activity in his brain these past twenty-four hours. I'm going to be honest, it doesn't look good. His pupils are dilated, and he's lacking respiratory reflexes. I'm really sorry to say, keeping him on life support will only prolong the inevitable."

"I understand," Patricia said. "I deal with cases like this in the nursing home all the time, but...this is my son. He's only twenty-five years old. I just can't—"

"I'll give you some time to think about it," the doctor said. Digging under his white jacket, he pulled out a radio pager, which informed him through static to report to the west wing. The doctor nodded his head and left, the door banging to a close behind him.

Patricia held her head in her hands. She peered over at her son who remained lost in a catastrophic slumber, his face a mess of cuts and bruises. His blond hair, typically parted down the middle, was brushed across his forehead. His arms rested by his sides, holding the white sheet in place.

"He can hear us, Jim. I know he can. They all do, you know. We'll just tell him to come back to us. He can't disobey his parents," Patricia said.

Jim's features softened, waves of wrinkles forming across his forehead. "We'll do as much as we can for him, Pat."

Returning to a standing position, Patricia nudged a stray penny across the floor with her foot. Reaching into her bag, she pulled out the old bear that she had given him for his fifth birthday. "Look, Jimmy, I brought you Balboa," she said. She held the stuffed animal over him before placing it at the top of his bed.

Jimmy's face remained serene. The room was silent aside from the monitor, marking the seconds that passed. Just as she couldn't bear the stillness any longer, her son's arm twitched before assuming its prior position on the sheet.

"Did you just see that, Jim? He moved! My Lord, he moved," Patricia cried.

Jim hurried beside her. They peered down at Jimmy who had settled back into a comatose state. Patricia waited, her eyes widening with eagerness. A half hour passed, then another. Her anticipation dissolved. Hope was a yank within, a flood of delight and disarray. Hope surfaced and went silent. A false, beeping alarm.

Wednesday -- February 4th -- 11:48 a.m.

They had not killed him, Patricia assured herself. When the life support was unplugged, he simply did not take to breathing or a heart beat on his own. It was all the decision of his body: brain waves ceasing, and the blood no longer flowing. The doctor had explained the twitch as a movement arising in the spinal cord and not from the brain.

Patricia scanned Jimmy's bedroom. It appeared as though he'd be returning at any moment. The blue comforter lay in a heap on his bed. Shirts, jeans, and socks formed a mountain of laundry in the middle of the floor. The basket beside his closet was still packed with dirty clothes. On his computer, the screen saver flashed landscapes from around the world. With a click of the mouse, Patricia found an open document displaying a graph half filled with numbers.

On the walls hung several posters: an orange AC/DC print; a close-up of Tiger Woods crouching beside a golf ball; a blurred image of running sneakers, laces undone in the shadows. There was a big screen TV perched atop an entertainment center, which was filled with a PlayStation and a DVD player. DVDs were scattered across the floor below.

"I don't know where to begin," Patricia said, her hands on her hips. If only she could preserve this scene so that he would always be on his way home. Patricia grabbed a shirt from the floor, holding it against her cheek. It smelled strongly of her son's cologne.

With the help of Jimmy's girlfriend, Sarah, and their roommates, Eddie and Brad, Jim unfolded the boxes they had picked up from a nearby liquor store to transfer Jimmy's belongings back to Massachusetts.

"Looks like a tornado hit this place," Jim mumbled. He wrapped the movies and CDs with newspaper before packing them into a box.

"Well you know how much he hated cleaning," Patricia said. "Remember the time he threw all of his clothes out the window to fool us into thinking he'd picked up his room? I think he was nine then." She folded another shirt from the floor. Instead of packing it, she placed it carefully onto the bed. Beside her, Eddie shut down the computer, unraveling the wires knotted together under the desk.

"He would avoid cleaning here, too," Sarah said as she removed the pictures from the walls. "I made the guys write lists of how they helped clean each day. I remember the first thing he wrote was, 'Cleared spider from the wall.' Nothing compared to my job of scrubbing the toilet, but I'm sure glad I didn't have to go after that gross bug!" She laughed quietly, shaking her head.

Patricia let loose a smile. "He always found a way around things he didn't want to do. Then, when you least expected it, he'd turn around and vacuum the whole house."

"He certainly was a trickster like that," Jim said.

"But he was clever in a considerate sort of way. It made it hard for me to get mad at him," Patricia said. Just as she reached for more dirty laundry from the floor, the doorbell rang. Brad hurried to answer it.

A minute later, he returned, Denise stumbling behind him with a small suitcase rolling at her heels. Her brown hair was tied into a bun, loose strands falling around her face. Her makeup was smudged at the corners of her eyes, emphasizing their round brown shape. Denise embraced her father before moving on to Patricia, who held on until her daughter backed away. Jimmy's friends stepped forward to share their condolences.

Patricia attempted to talk, but stopped, the words trapped behind her lips.

"Your trip go okay?" Jim asked finally, half looking at the floor.

Denise pushed down the handle of her suitcase, lowering her head. "Yeah I just—I can't believe I missed him. I didn't even say goodbye."

Patricia choked back tears. She pulled out a torn-up tissue from her pocket, still damp from earlier, and dabbed her eyes. "I know. I'm sorry. Everything's happening so fast," she said. Gazing at her daughter, she admired the boldness of Denise's features despite the watery glaze building over her eyes. In some ways, Denise was identical to her son. She possessed the same thin, pointed nose accenting her high cheekbones. Although her skin too was a soft milky white, Denise's features were darker, like her father's. Her eyes exuded a polite confidence, which Jimmy had only begun to develop four years behind her.

"You can put your luggage in the living room if you want. Your mom and I stayed at a hotel down the street so we can bring it over later when we're done," Jim said.

"Sure."

The floor cleared, Patricia gathered the dirty clothes from Jimmy's bed and piled them inside the laundry basket for Eddie to take to the machines.

"Sarah was just talking about how nice Jimmy was to wipe away the bugs crawling around here," Patricia said.

Her daughter's gaze extended across the room. Denise's tears had ceased, but Patricia noted a shred of despair buried beneath her daughter's sturdy look.

"Oh man, don't get me started. You remember he used to

give me cups full of potato bugs for my birthday. I guess he never grew out of that," Denise said.

Patricia pulled on the dragonfly pendant hanging under her cotton shirt that her son had given her for Christmas. She grasped it tight in her hand, careful enough not to bend its green mesh wings. The blue curtains fluttered into the air before settling back against the windowpane. A warm, fresh breeze filled the room with the faint scent of roses.

"Who opened the window?" Patricia asked.

Jim looked up at her. He had just finished packing most of the accessories scattered around the entertainment center. "I don't know," he said. "I think it was already open." Picking up a piece of newspaper, he held in the other hand a picture of Jimmy on his motorcycle.

"He loved that thing," Brad said. "Used to take it for a ride every day after class. Sometimes he wouldn't come back until it was just barely getting dark. Always enjoyed driving into the sunset."

Patricia cleared her throat. "You know the story behind it? He begged us for that motorcycle for his twenty-first birthday. And when I refused to get it for him, he saved up his money even after the move here. Even after reminding him he was moving way too far away from home."

"Moving to California was his dream though," Eddie said. "He told us constantly about his plan to open a restaurant on the water, but he wasn't sure if he could do it. He was always gushing about how much he loved it here."

Denise sat down on the computer chair, dangling her arm over the top. "No doubt about that. Remember when he left home early last fall because he missed California so much?"

"Because Patricia made him clean up after himself," Jim said.

"He made it all the way through this Christmas vacation with us though. Thank goodness," Patricia replied. She noticed Jimmy's girlfriend huddled in one corner of the room, knees folded to her chest with her back against the wall. Tears glided down her face.

"He knew he belonged here. He couldn't quite explain—" Sarah cut herself off.

Stripping the sheets from the bed, Patricia piled them on the floor. She sat down on the bare mattress, looking around. Everyone had stopped moving, each person's focus lingering in a different direction. The birds sang pleasant tunes, which carried through the window. Everyone remained silent, lost in their own hushed daze.

Thursday -- February 5th -- 1:25 a.m.

Patricia lay beside her husband, back in their own bed. Jim rested on his back, one arm folded behind his head, mouth open. He released sessions of snoring, which fizzled out into a soft whining in his nose. Just as Patricia was finally beginning to doze off, the phone beside her bed rang into her ears. She shot up, her heart beating fast.

Jim twitched, but remained asleep.

Reaching for the receiver, Patricia glanced at the clock lit up in red numerals. One thirty-nine.

"Hello?" Soft static hummed on the other end. "Hello? Anyone there? Guess not. In case you didn't know, 1:30am is not the best time for prank calls, asshole," she said, slamming down the phone.

Patricia dropped her head to the pillow. Though her body ached from exhaustion, the events of the past week replayed in her mind. She saw her son attached to breathing tubes, the line on the screen remaining flat. She heard the conversations with the doctors.

"Your son is a known donor, Mr. and Mrs. Pollaski. His heart, his lungs, and his kidneys will go to people in need of new organs."

"People will get to live because of him," Jim had answered.

The idea of helping others filled her with gratitude, only until the realization of its expense hit once again.

How can we just give away our child? Patricia thought. *Only twenty-five years old.*

Patricia cursed as she shifted to her right side, then to her left again, before settling onto her back. After what seemed like hours, her mind calmed. Falling into a deep sleep, she dreamed she was airborne among birds and organ-like images. A human heart with enormous white-feathered wings fluttered by her in a sky of deep blue. Although it didn't have a face, it spoke. "People will clean and move out, but they do check in at another hotel," it said. Patricia soared along, saying nothing. When she awoke, she remembered only of having dreamed something she could not recover in her mind.

Rubbing her eyes, Patricia lifted her head away from the sunlight filtering through the curtains. Jim's side of the bed was empty. Pulling herself upright, she focused on the unopened envelopes resting on top of the desk. Inside were the papers from the hospital they had received the previous day: a copy of the death certificate signed by the doctor, and an employment identification number in replacement of her son's social security number, to be used for his final tax return.

Patricia turned toward the closet. She grabbed the first outfit she could find within reach—a long-sleeved black shirt and some wrinkled jeans. Throwing her pajamas onto the floor, she changed and headed out into the hallway, tucking the envelope under her arm.

"Jim, could you come up here, please?" Patricia called. Downstairs, the television blared.

Although Jim didn't answer, the TV turned off. Waiting, she clutched the top of the railing, one foot on the step below. As he appeared, Patricia turned her back toward him, then moved forward, opening the door to Jimmy's childhood bedroom directly overlooking the staircase.

"We have to pick an outfit for him," she said.

Jim stopped before entering the room. "An outfit? You know I'm not too good at that."

"He would've liked knowing it was you who chose the non-matching one. I'll help you, anyway. We need to do this together."

"I suppose you're right," he said.

They stared at the boxes, which had not yet been touched. Cutting the tape from the box she had marked "Clothing," Patricia sifted through several pairs of jeans, t-shirts, and collared shirts. She couldn't remember seeing her son in any of the clothes, even though some looked familiar from the day she had cleaned his room.

"What about this one?" Jim asked, holding up a blue and black striped dress shirt. "Didn't he wear this on Christmas?"

"I think he did."

"Why not this one?"

Patricia nodded. "I think so." She dug to the bottom of the box where she found a blue t-shirt that matched the piercing blue of Jimmy's eyes. In a smaller box, he kept his high school graduation ring, a shell necklace Patricia had made for him before he moved to California, and a picture of him and his dog from when he was a kid. Finding some gray slacks to match, she tossed them into a bag.

"Let's go. We should probably leave for the funeral home. Our appointment's in thirty minutes," she said. She headed out of the bedroom, Jim closing the door behind them.

Saturday -- February 7th -- 11:15 a.m.

The dreary New England days passed quickly, leading into the hour of Jimmy's funeral. A group of his friends stood together beside the tall oak tree, its bare branches hanging over the site. A crow perched on one branch cawed into the sky. Behind them, rows of stones stretched over the hill. So many people came forth to express their sorrow, some Patricia didn't even recognize.

The minister's voice echoed in the still air. "It is always hard to understand why God must take our children from the world so soon, with so many plans ahead of them."

Patricia lowered her head, staring into the dirt. From the corner of her eye, she saw her mother's and father's stones. Patricia held her breath, releasing it when she could no longer bear the lack of oxygen. The warmth of her husband's arm against her own, and her daughter's hand on her shoulder, assured her that the rest of her family was not far away. Her young granddaughter's whine filtered through the minister's dialogue.

My son, my baby. Right here in front of me, yet gone, Patricia thought. Her tears, stunted in the earlier hours of the day, now flowed beyond her control. The minister handed them each a white rose. They tossed the roses onto the closed box. It was nearly over, as the day proceeded to pass away.

CHAPTER TWO

Lorrena Shaw

Monday -- February 2nd -- 6:48 p.m.

Her homework sat on her desk, neglected. Lorrena instead scribbled in her journal, her hatred of the homework that was unnecessary for her future. The beach on a chilly February night beat calculating limits anyway, diverting her attention from numerical devices and the eerie voices in her head, which gave no answers.

Lorrena let her thoughts flow free to the page. When was the last time she had seen the moon slice the sky, its reflection shining over the water? Why did she not understand the math equations? Her memories of watching the waves crash over the rocks had faded, but why were the ghostly images that she saw in her mind so clear?

Lorrena put down her pen. The smell of fish patties drifted up the stairs to her room. The idea of fresh air swept over her. Grabbing her jacket, mittens, and scarf from the floor beneath her bed, Lorrena bundled herself up before she climbed out of her window. She slid down slowly against the house, onto the roof of the addition below. The ground always looked far from there, but it was a jump Lorrena had handled fine many times before. She carefully unhooked Godiva, her chocolate lab, from the run before heading toward Gonya Cove. Her breath cut smoke across the night air.

It was a short walk until the road speckled with houses turned into trees, transforming into a rock wall, into sand dunes. Making her way past the "Private: No Trespassing" sign, Lorrena chased Godiva across wet, sinking sand, leaving behind deformed footprints as she stepped into the unbroken surface ahead.

Lorrena stared out across the water. The dark sky merged with the ocean, the sun having disappeared hours ago. The moon, full in size, hung above the mansions on the right side of the shore. Like the moon and stars dotting the sky, the houses also provided light as the residents ate their meals beneath sparkling chandeliers. The buildings towered over the ocean, acting as the watch guards of Connecticut's secluded shores.

Lorrena stopped running, catching her breath on the upper part of the beach. The cold air stung her cheeks. She held her mittens against her face. Lowering herself into the sand, Lorrena spied into the windows bordered with lace curtains. They allowed her an ideal view of the families serving dinner over their perfect white tablecloths.

"Maybe someday they'll ask us to join," Lorrena said out loud, patting her dog's brown fur. Godiva licked her face. "Even though Mom would have no one to yell at, she might not even care that we were gone."

Just as Lorrena settled herself against a rock, a cold wind

swept sand into the air. The sudden chill nipped at her skin, sending a surge of uneasiness through her body. Lorrena gazed toward the left side of the coast, the woods thick and monstrous at the beach's edge. Squinting, she caught sight of a dull glow penetrating through the shadows.

Lorrena shut her eyes. When she opened them again, the light vanished as quickly as it had appeared.

She remembered the first time a ghost had manifested before her. As a four-year-old, visions had kept her alert with tears into the early hours of the morning. Her mother's invitation to sleep in her bed comforted Lorrena only until the lights were off. Twelve years of sleeping with the lights on had not altered her ability to see so well in the dark. She stood without moving, watching intently as the silhouette re-emerged, this time closer.

"They love these old buildings," Lorrena said. Godiva growled at the trees. An upheaval of barking echoed over the beach as her dog took off toward the stone wall.

"Godiva, get back here! It's only a stupid ghost. Just let her be!" Lorrena yelled. She stood, sprinting after her dog. The closer she got, the clearer the shape became. The radiance materialized into the form of a woman dressed in an old-fashioned gown, her expression distraught.

Grabbing her dog's collar, Lorrena yanked Godiva toward the beach's entrance. Her dog pulled her forward. Lorrena closed her eyes for a moment, the image disappearing once again. She listened to the wind playing tunes through the tree branches. The freedom from her powers never lasted very long.

"*Carl, come back to me, please. Come back,*" the woman cried in a frequency only Lorrena and her dog's ears picked up. She heard the voices, like an intrusive sound ricocheting in her head. It was as if her brain had tuned into a radio broadcast possessing no tangible controls.

Lorrena sang out loud, her song accompanied by barking.

"*Carl, I beg of you. Don't you leave me here alone. I can't handle it without you. I need you.*" The ghost's shrill cries blended with her weeping.

Lorrena headed back down the beach. Just as the voice died out, another light surfaced at the opening of the street.

"Get out of here, girl!" Lorrena heard someone say, but this time the sound came from outside of her skull.

"Stop talking to me," Lorrena yelled, clasping her hands over her ears. Her head ached from shutting her eyes so hard. "I've had enough of this! Just leave me alone!"

An abrupt tap on the shoulder brought Lorrena back to reality. A woman holding a flashlight glared at her. Godiva wagged her tail, whining.

"Are you crazy? Get the hell out of here! Don't you know this is private property? I could've easily called the cops on you! Now run along, before you get yourself into trouble!" the woman yelled. She planted one hand on her hip, the other pointing the flashlight toward the road.

"I'm so sorry. We were just admiring the view. We'll leave," Lorrena said. "Here, girl. Let's go. This way."

Lorrena rushed home, singing softly under her breath. As she approached her house, her mother, Erin, appeared in the open doorway dressed in a dirtied apron.

"Lorrena Shaw, what in the world are you doing out here? Get inside before you catch pneumonia. I don't know who gave you permission to roam around out here when you should be doing homework, but it clearly wasn't me!"

Lorrena ushered her dog through the door, slamming it behind them. "You can't tell me what to do, Mom. I'm not your child anymore. I'm sixteen years old!"

"You will always be my child. Don't give me that."

Lorrena walked to the sink, soaking her numb, aching fingers under warm water. Her mother's nagging persisted—the importance of obeying the house rules, how she was not yet an official adult. Lorrena's concentration remained elsewhere as the ramblings of a ghost who had taken up residence in the laundry room resounded in her ears. This ghost, who Lorrena called Edna after a housemaid character she'd read in a book, was known for spilling detergent onto the floor, and dropping clean clothes behind the dryer. No matter her innocence, Lorrena always took the blame.

"Don't forget to put out the fire, Bobby, I ain't doin' ya dirty work no more!" Edna's voice crooned.

"I just don't want you going out after it gets late, okay? That's all I'm saying."

"It's barely eight at night, Mom," she said, pointing to the clock above the sink.

"I don't care what time it is, Lorrena. It's dark outside, especially in the woods. Dinner is getting cold. I've been waiting here scared out of my mind, no idea where you went. For all I know, you could've be dead somewhere."

Lorrena chuckled. "Oh, I'd definitely let you know if I were dead," she muttered under her breath.

"Excuse me? I'm not in the mood for your attitude, and I certainly don't want to hear any more of that crazy nonsense." She shot Lorrena a stern look as she removed her apron. "Come on, dinner is ready." Erin turned and headed toward the dining room, which was lit with two thick red candles smelling of cherries. Lorrena reluctantly followed.

"I told you I would get you some help," Erin said. She pulled out a chair and sat down while Lorrena stood in silence, staring at her plate of soggy food. "You don't have to deal with those awful hallucinations, Lorrena. If you accept that what you're seeing isn't real, then you'll be able to conquer them."

"I don't want to talk about it, Mom," Lorrena said. "Is it okay if I eat upstairs?" She could still hear Edna's voice reverberating from behind the wall.

"*Put out the fire now, Bobby!*"

"I'd really like it if you'd sit with me," her mother said.

"*Listen here, Bobby, you do what you're told or else!*"

Lorrena turned to face where she believed Edna to be. "Quiet!" she shouted. Cupping her hand around her mouth, she added to her mother, "Sorry, intended for Edna."

Erin stopped her fork mid-bite without responding. Lorrena waited for another snide remark, but her mother remained composed. Finally, she looked up at Lorrena, her eyebrows raised. "Well? Are you going to stand there and argue with invisible people all night, or are you going to sit down and eat your dinner?"

Lorrena kept her mouth shut. Her mother's cheeks turned crimson with anger as if she were still standing outside in the cold.

"I actually have some important things to tell you, Lorrena. Stuff that'll affect your future. I'd appreciate it if you sat down."

"I'll sit, but I won't eat this."

For the next minute, the only sounds Lorrena heard were her mother's fork against the glassware. The wind knocking at the door, and the snapping of the fire in the woodstove.

"Well?" Lorrena asked, impatient.

"We're moving out of town."

Lorrena's mouth fell open. "I'm sorry, but did you just

say that we're moving?"

"Yes, I did. We'll most likely be out of here by the end of the month, at the latest."

"But it's almost my last year of high school. I have friends here. Why would you want to leave? Dad rebuilt this house for us."

"I know it's your junior year, but we have to."

Her mother continued to shove food into her mouth as if words she didn't approve of would escape.

"Because why?" Lorrena asked again.

Her mother swallowed. Looking Lorrena straight in the face, her reply was as sharp as her stare. "You have a grandmother, Lorrena. My mother. She's sick. We're going to help take care of her."

"I have a *what*? A grandmother? No, I don't believe you. There's just no way."

"You don't have to believe me, but it's the truth," Erin said. Her fork rang against her plate as it dropped.

"But I don't understand. Why am I only learning this now, after so many years? Why wasn't she there when I was born? Or at Christmas or any other holiday for that matter?"

"I wish I had an answer for that."

"Right. You have absolutely no explanation why I've grown up without knowing my grandmother," Lorrena said, crossing her arms. "Or why I have to leave the only house I've ever lived in. I really think I deserve these details after sixteen years in the dark. The dark, Mom! Didn't you just finish lecturing me on how dangerous it is?"

Erin slammed her fist against the table. "Now is not the time, okay? We're moving, and that is final."

Lorrena stood, knocking the table with her hip. She threw her napkin down over her food. "Okay. Well, I think it's time I go upstairs to finish my homework. Not like it even matters now." She turned and marched through the living room.

Crossing over the smooth, wood floor, Lorrena admired the pleasant coziness of their dwelling—the only home she'd ever known. Handmade quilts draped over the wooden couches made of the same tailored timber as the immense bookcases, which were packed to the brim with old, dusty books. Intricate woodworking was carved into each piece of wooden furniture. Flowered drapes hung across rows of windows, a chain of picture frames resting along the windowsills; portraits of her mother, and her father holding a five-year-old Lorrena in his arms, just before he had died; Godiva as a small ball of chocolate fur. But now as she passed by, her family portraits appeared different—happy, yet incomplete.

Lorrena's stomach whined. She yanked on the railing, pulling herself up the blue-carpeted stairs to her room. Her desk lamp, casting shadows of her pencil jar onto her homework and her blue-and-white striped journal, lit her own special space. She glanced briefly at the unfinished math problems before placing her forehead down on the desk.

"As X approaches infinity, the value of the function is crushed by my head, not wanting to calculate anything except the miles to my new home, wherever this grandmother of mine may be," she mumbled under her breath.

After a few minutes, Lorrena lifted her left hand to her ear, propping her head up with her elbow. She picked up a pencil, jotting her thoughts down in her journal. She did not want to abandon the house where she'd grown up, leaving her friends and her school behind. But there was so much more to learn about this new family member. How old was she? How gray had her hair become? Maybe Lorrena and her mother had both inherited the same dark, boisterous hair from her grandmother. Perhaps the light blue color of Lorrena's eyes, absent from those of her parents, was a gift from the old woman. Aside from being the mother of her mother, who was she exactly? Where had her years been spent, in the absence of a daughter? What if she had fallen ill from a broken heart, the disappearance of her descendants throbbing inside her? What if her heartache had developed into a lifelong head cold? She was probably sick of simply not knowing, tired from years of guessing. Or maybe she was bubbling with life—one of those hip grandmothers who took their grandchildren on 24-hour shopping excursions. Or was she on the verge of death? Maybe her grandmother had known of *her* all along.

Lorrena's mind drifted in circles, contemplating why her father had never mentioned her grandmother. He visited Lorrena often, mostly at night, his image emerging like a reflection in the water, whispering things she couldn't quite understand. Then he disappeared.

Lorrena changed quickly into her pajamas before climbing into bed, without even brushing her teeth.

The day's clutter filtered through her head as the voices returned again. Her power to dismiss them drifted into oblivion, as her body grew closer to sleep. Her stomach growled. Lorrena's comprehension subsided, the sounds lulling her into a familiar world of dreams that she would not remember in the morning.

CHAPTER THREE

Patricia Pollaski

Monday -- February 18th -- 2:08 p.m.

P atricia rushed across the living room. She slammed the window closed, trapping the frosty air between the glass and the ice-spattered screen. She couldn't remember opening it. Months ago she had reminded her husband to replace the summer screens with the storm windows since the house had taken on a wintry chill. Jim's bulky winter parka hung beside the door while he trekked around outside, braving the twenty-degree weather in layers of flannel shirts. His boots remained tucked away in the closet, stuffed with his gloves and hat.

There was no one else living in the house now besides the two of them—an old married couple still together after thirty-four years. As Patricia listened to the thick silence, the absence of her offspring mounted—a daughter given away to marriage, a son lost to disaster. Had it really been twenty years since her children were at play, tossing snowballs at the windows? Patricia closed her eyes, squeezing out one tear, which made it only until the top of her cheek before she wiped it away. She recalled Jimmy as a six-year-old, his hat nearly pulled over his eyes as he launched a ball of ice at his sister, laughing. Missing Denise's face by inches, it flew by her, shattering the window where Patricia watched, pieces of glass falling to the floor beneath her feet.

Patricia dropped onto the couch, leaning her head back against its soft cushions as she released a heavy sigh.

"Don't start this again," she muttered aloud. "If you sit down you won't ever want to get up." After a few moments, she pulled herself to a standing position. Turning toward the staircase, her eyes stalled at the window, catching a view of the yard enclosed with bare trees. She thought of the advice from everyone within the past few weeks. The importance of keeping busy despite the urge to freeze mid-breath. The need to release her emotions instead of bottling them up inside. And what her sister in-law stressed most: not blaming herself for what had happened.

Patricia hiked up the stairs to Jimmy's bedroom. Aside from a twin bed and a dresser, the room had remained empty since his move-out until now, many accessories having found their way back home without him. Earlier that week, her husband insisted she sort through his things, deciding which items to keep in his memory. The rest would be donated to charity. Patricia, awkwardly perched atop a cardboard box, spent the next hour examining the room. Taking note of the boxes, she compared their rigid surfaces with the empty gray walls behind them. There were seven packages wrapped in mailing tape, including the one they had searched the previous day, taped back up. Three boxes of favored memorabilia she had dismissed into his roommates' possession: cooking utensils, his old golfing equipment and hockey gear, a *Fight Club* DVD, and a copy of Stephen King's *The Shining*.

Patricia observed her watch's hands as they shifted and hesitated, turning inconspicuously in circles. It was now 3:34pm. When she found no urge to move forward, she gathered just enough energy to lift herself to her feet, only to fall back down a second later, unable to bear the thought of ripping off the tape tightly bound to the cardboard panels. Finally she stood, her knees locking. The room spun. Her head, heavy, collapsed in her hands.

Her 25-year-old boy was no longer alive, a fact she couldn't quite comprehend. She felt somewhere inside her that it just couldn't be so. Perhaps he was still going about his daily routine three thousand miles away in San Diego. He'd be picking up the phone any minute after his shift at the restaurant, after his class at San Diego State University, or his run on the beach, to call her. The phone remained silent.

Patricia rubbed her eyes, leaving her son's room. She closed the door gently behind her and trudged back down the stairs. Instead of vacuuming up the crumbs her husband had left on the floor earlier that morning, she fell down onto the couch, reaching for her purse. Inside was a photograph that Brad had given her. The snapshot revealed a mere instant of Jimmy's final week of life. In the corner of the picture, Eddie held two fishing rods against his body. Jimmy was caught mid-dive, just past the pier's wooden railing, the ocean below him.

Patricia looked at the picture for what seemed like hours, as if it were a TV show stuck on pause. Squeezing her eyes shut, she tried to imagine what Jimmy would look like at this very moment if he were still alive. All she could envision was an indefinite image of her son years ago, merging with how he had last looked as he waved goodbye from the airport a few months earlier. As a boy, he had grown up so fast. His blond hair hanging askew over eager blue eyes, which squinted as he observed faraway scenes. His tall, lanky body. How he possessed a knack for any sport. How he was always filled with so much energy.

Patricia held the picture close to her face. It wavered in the air, shaking with her hand. The wind knocked at the windows as remnants of cool air touched her arms, and she shivered. Just as she tucked the picture into her wallet, the door burst open behind her, lifting her blonde hair from her shoulders.

"Really not too bad out there," her husband shouted. "Certainly not at all like the California weather, but I swear, once you get below thirty degrees it all starts to feel the same." She didn't turn around to meet him face to face. As he walked toward her, she saw out of the corner of her eye the path his muddy sneakers had formed across the brown tile.

"What are you talking about, Jim? It's below freezing. And you're not even wearing your jacket! Are you trying to catch pneumonia?"

"Of course not," Jim said. "It's only a little bit of cold air. It's refreshing. Stop worrying, I'll be fine."

"What do you mean, stop worrying? We're not in California anymore. If you're going on some Alaskan adventure, take your gear with you and please don't bring the slush back inside the house," she said.

Jim sat down in the armchair, slipping off his sneakers as more melted snow dripped onto the floor. "I'm sorry. I didn't mean to upset you," he said, brushing the sneakers aside with his foot. Crossing his arms behind his head, the footrest popped open as the chair reclined backward. He closed his eyes, but continued to speak. "The nursing home called yesterday. Did you get the message?" he asked. "I don't see why you couldn't have answered the phone. I mean, you haven't even left the house these past few weeks."

"I don't know what you're talking about. I didn't hear the phone ring. I must've been out shopping or something." She pulled her purse back into her lap and pretended to sift through it.

"They have your paycheck waiting for you. Something about the director wanting to talk to you," he mumbled.

"Oh, of course. I'll have to listen to the message soon."

Jim lifted his head. As he did, Patricia met his gaze for a moment before she turned to look out the window.

"Have you thought about going back to work?" he asked.

Patricia realized that she hadn't considered returning to work, regardless of people's advice. She hoped to spend her days in the near future at home, resting from the pressure of everyday exertion. Since the funeral, she'd spent her time buried beneath a book or watching soap operas. Yet the easygoing hours of the day drained her.

"Yes, I have thought about it," Patricia lied. "But—I thought I'd be much happier getting some work done around the house. You know? Because why rush getting back into the swing of things?"

Gliding his hands through his brown hair, a few gray strands fell back over his eyes before he closed them again. "Tomorrow you should go," he said.

Patricia nodded, even though he couldn't see her.

Thursday -- February 19ᵗʰ -- 1:20 p.m.

The sign advertising Kendall Retirement in bold blue letters emerged from behind a large oak tree as Patricia rounded the corner. The facility, pushed back from the street by a long pathway lined with bushes, possessed a friendly yet secluded atmosphere which Patricia believed made it the premier assisted living center in the city of Gloucester.

She passed through the front door, initiating the doorbell. Assembled around the small circular table, she found a few women talking casually and sipping tea. Patricia recognized Mrs. Adelphie and Mrs. Grand, but couldn't identify the third woman in the wheelchair.

"Hello, ladies," Patricia said.

The women waved at her, smiling with enthusiasm.

"How are you doing?" Mrs. Adelphie asked. "Haven't seen you 'round this place in a while. We were a bit concerned about you."

Patricia forced a smile. "Well, I'm here now. No need to worry."

"Why, yes of course," the old woman said. "Care to join us for some tea?"

Patricia craned her neck to see inside the small office built into the back wall of the lobby. "Oh, I'm sorry. No time today. Just came to speak quickly with Mrs. Marietta."

"As you wish." The smile from Mrs. Adelphie's face dissolved. "I believe she's in the office."

Patricia put her hand on the woman's shoulder. "I'll be back soon. We'll have tea and catch up, I promise."

She stepped backward before spinning around into the office. Sitting at the desk to Patricia's left, the director had her

28

nose buried in a manila folder. Mrs. Marietta was a woman bubbly in temperament who appeared much older than her actual age, somewhere in her late fifties. Over the many years Patricia had been working with her, the lady had accumulated a full head of gray hair and a tendency to be hard of hearing. The woman spent so much time around older people that she had inadvertently taken up characteristics of a person going into retirement herself.

Finally looking up from her work after a minute of deep concentration, Mrs. Marietta raised her chin in Patricia's direction. Her face lit up.

"Ah, my dear, here you are." Her reading glasses perched on the bottom of her nose accentuated the magnitude of her eyes. She strolled around the desk, her shoulders hunched over until she raised her arms up. She hugged Patricia the way a mother delicately embraces a small child, although Patricia knew the woman had no children of her own. "I'm so sorry to hear about your son," Mrs. Marietta said. "Take as much time as you need for yourself, though everyone does miss you very much. All has gone crazy in your absence."

Patricia pressed her lips firmly together. She glanced at the old ladies who sat without shifting. She pictured herself sitting the same way on top of the boxes.

"Please don't feel pressured. Losing your child is devastating, and we want you to fully recover before you return to work. For your health, especially," Mrs. Marietta said, patting her on the shoulder.

"I can start again next week."

Mrs. Marietta's features softened. "Ah, God bless you. You are doing a great favor to the men and women here."

A smile slipped across Patricia's face. At the same time, she blinked away tears building behind her eyelids.

"I'm so glad you're doing well." Mrs. Marietta waved her arms around as she spoke in a high-pitched tone. "I know that with all of the bad news you've been receiving, you'll be glad to hear we've gained three new residents and have only lost one. One of the new women, in her 80s, gets along quite well on her own but experiences occasional memory loss. There's a gentleman who recently lost his wife, can't take care of himself on his own, and is devastated without his spouse of sixty years. The second new lady holds incredibly intelligent conversations when you least expect it. You'll get to meet them all next week, so I'll spare you any more synopses."

"Thank you so much for understanding, Mrs. Marietta," Patricia said. She grabbed her paycheck out of the staff box and waved goodbye.

On her way out, Patricia stopped to speak to the old women. "I'll see you all next week," she said.

"Goodbye, Mrs. Pollaski," Mrs. Adelphie said.

Mrs. Grand smiled back. The lady in the wheelchair beside her, who had appeared to be lost in a daze, looked Patricia in the eye.

"Take care. And remember, all is a natural part of life," the woman said, grasping the wheels of her chair.

Unsure of what to say, Patricia nodded. With a quick wave, she headed out the door, the bell ringing in her ears.

CHAPTER FOUR

Lorrena Shaw

Sunday -- February 22nd -- 1:30 p.m.

L orrena called to her dog, her voice rumbling through the empty living room. The movers had taken everything except the wooden couch frame, an end table, and the boxes she had spent hours filling with books, picture frames, quilts, and her mother's dusty tapestries.

Lorrena stood with her arms at her sides, listening for the clink of Godiva's tags. The windows stripped of curtains displayed the evergreens and the oaks rising above the fence in her backyard. All she could hear were the movers loading the furniture from her mother's room into the truck, combined with her mother's shouts. The voices in her mind subsided as she concentrated only on the external sounds.

Sitting down on one of the boxes, Lorrena dug her elbows

into her knees, resting her head in her hands. Strands of her dark, wavy hair fell from behind her ears. She left the pieces hanging by her face as she observed the nearly vacant room. It was strange how the room appeared so much smaller. How the walls she had once thought looked white, were pale blue in the sunlight. How the stains on the carpets became visible. Since her father's death, her mother had kept the curtains closed all day and night.

Nearly three weeks had passed since her mother's confession, which slowly settled in her stomach. It was not until now that Lorrena began to fully digest what she'd heard. They were moving. Leaving behind the house her dad had rebuilt, just for them. Anxiety filled Lorrena's chest each night, allowing her only a few hours of sleep. Yet the idea of change opened her up to a world of possibilities. The hope of meeting new friends. Fresh ground to explore with her dog. A woman of her own flesh and blood she had never even seen in pictures. Lorrena tensed up as she heard her mother's boots clunk through the kitchen.

"Lorrena! What are you doing just sitting there? Get up and make yourself useful!" Erin ordered.

"I finished packing up all the boxes, Mom," Lorrena said, hopping to her feet. "What else do you want me to do?"

"They have to get this stuff out to the truck somehow." Her mother stopped and thought for a moment. "I know. Why don't you help me move the couch to the door?" She measured a few steps with her boots.

Lorrena eyed the hallway, which wrapped around the bend to the left, forming a semi-circle to the door. She frowned.

"Oh, I don't know, twenty, thirty feet? I think we got it," her mother said.

Lorrena put her hands on her hips. "Isn't this what the movers are here for?"

"Don't be such a pill. It's your stuff they're moving, isn't it? You can't give them a hand?"

"Fine." Lorrena secured her grip around the couch's wooden base. The thick cushion still rested on top of the couch as her mother raised one side slowly to test the weight.

"We can do this," Erin urged. "It's not too bad."

"Yeah, that's what you told me last week before I almost fell down the stairs with my bookshelf."

"I can have them drop your things off at the dump if you'd like."

Lorrena rolled her eyes. She lifted the couch as her mother dragged her side along the floor.

"Don't worry, I got it," Lorrena said in her most sarcastic tone. Her arms shook as she stepped backward. She observed the wood floor passing beneath her feet, but raised her head up when Edna's translucent figure appeared. The ghost floated above the couch as it moved. Her face formed a curious look, her arms folded across her chest.

"Keep going, almost there," her mother said.

Lorrena focused on the ghost. "What do you think this is? An amusement ride?" she muttered. She shifted her feet faster around the wide corner as they approached the doorway. Edna stared out into the distance, unresponsive to Lorrena's comment.

Lorrena could no longer feel her fingers.

"Quick, Mom, drop it. My hands are slipping," she called out, releasing her end of the couch. She shook her hands out in relief as her mother stumbled backward.

"Dammit! Right on my foot, Lorrena. You've got to be more careful!" Erin bent down to clutch her ankle.

"Whose bright idea was it to move the couch in the first place?" Lorrena asked, watching Edna's lucid form float through the glass window. The ghost vanished as it reached the driveway where the movers had just finished packing the bedroom furniture.

"Well, maybe if you weren't talking to imaginary people! Sixteen years old, you'd think you would've grown out of it by now."

"Edna was right there, Mom. It's not my fault you're forty something and blind."

"Lorrena Shaw, please don't speak to me like that," her mother said. She heatedly adjusted her cashmere sweater, creases forming between her eyebrows. It was her mother's usual response when she became irritated. Lorrena waited for the headshake followed by a loud groan before she responded.

"I'll bet the movers packed Edna into the truck too!"

Erin's cheeks turned pink. "Quiet, Lorrena. Cut the crap and let's just finish this job, okay? We don't have two years."

Before her mother finished her sentence, three of the movers entered the house. Behind them was her best friend from down the street, Ariel.

Ariel looked at Lorrena with an eyebrow raised, speaking silently to her friend with her eyes. The two had been neighbors for as long as Lorrena could remember, bouncing from door to door to escape the constraints of their own households. Ariel could always detect Lorrena's mother's 'battle face,' as she called it. The two exchanged glances, which Lorrena translated into, 'Back away, she's ready to explode.'

"Excuse me, Miss?" one of the movers spoke up, wiping his hands on his blue coveralls. "Do you want us to get that for you? Spare you the backache?"

"Well, we were doing fine," Lorrena's mother said. "But

yes, it would be nice to have some assistance, I guess. In fact, I'll direct you out the door. Oh, and hi Ariel, it's good to see you today. I'm glad you came to say goodbye to Lorrena before we leave."

"Hi, Mrs. Shaw," Ariel said, gritting her teeth at Lorrena.

Lorrena rushed to her friend's side. "I know, she thinks she's the boss of everyone," she whispered, watching her mother pointing as the movers hauled the couch out the door. "Let's go out back and check on my dog. I haven't heard her barking for a while."

Ariel nodded. Lorrena grabbed her jacket from the coat rack on the wall, leaving the wooden rungs bare. The girls hurried to the door in the back of the house, leading out to the deck.

Passing through the living room, Lorrena watched her friend's gaze dart in all directions as she eyed the house's emptiness.

"Wow. It looks so different in here. I don't even believe it," Ariel said as Lorrena shuffled in front of her.

"Yeah, isn't it sad? I've lived here my whole life. Rebuilt by my father's hands and Mom doesn't care in the least about putting it up for sale. I swear, ever since she told me about my grandmother, she's put up her walls." Lorrena fiddled with the lock until it clicked.

"Maybe your grandmother's more uptight than your Mom is, and she's scared."

Lorrena turned the knob, pushing open the door with her hip. She stepped forward slowly to ease herself into the frosty February air, rubbing her hands together to preserve heat. The early afternoon sun hid behind thick clouds, which had calmed within the past hours from spurts of snow flurries. She breathed in, the coldness burning her nose. The smell of fire lingered in the air. A chorus of barking rang out somewhere off in the distance.

Godiva answered back as the girls grew closer.

"Godey, hush!" Lorrena demanded. They traipsed across the icy deck, down the staircase to a small yard framed by a wooden fence. "There's no need to make such a ruckus."

Her dog bolted to her side and rested her head on Lorrena's knee as she squatted down. The dog's fur was damp, leaving wet spots on her jeans. A mass of loose hairs collected in her palm. Lorrena smiled, finding comfort in the familiar smell of her dog's coat dripping with moisture.

"So do you think your dog knows that something's going on?"

Lorrena waived her arms around as Godiva darted back and forth, following her lead. "Oh, of course. Dogs sense changes in the atmosphere very well, better than humans do. I bet Godiva knew we were moving before I did," she joked.

Ariel chuckled, but didn't reply. Tilting her head up, she raised her hands to the sky. "Maybe she'll tell you why you haven't met your grandmother," she said finally.

"My dog doesn't know *that* much." Lorrena laughed, following her friend's gaze. Snowflakes grazed the air like specks of dust, disintegrating as they hit the ground.

"No, I mean your mother, you dork."

"I know, I know," Lorrena said. "At dinner a few nights ago, I tried to ask her about the last time they'd seen each other. I told her if she didn't answer me I'd run away to Ohio and get a job working in the corn fields. All I got was a lecture on how not to talk with my mouth full of food and nonsense."

Ariel shook her head. "Mothers! I swear, they think they can get away with anything."

Lorrena nodded. She kicked a pile of soggy leaves, which

had clumped together after weeks of precipitation. The lawn was covered in patches of brown. The trees, once adorned in bright reds and golden browns, shed their leaves across the ground, the winter weather now having finished them off entirely.

Sighing, Lorrena shimmied backwards until her heels found the step, and she sat. "Don't you sometimes wish you could go back to those days when you were oblivious to everything? When you were so small, you had no idea the world existed beyond your family? When everything appeared so big and new?"

Ariel's shoulders shook as the wind tugged her blonde hair across her flushed face. She looked as if she were bathing in her big winter parka as the snow melted into her sleeves. "Yeah, tell me about it," she said.

"Back then, not once did I ever question my mother when we were alone at Christmas and Easter," Lorrena said, "or when every other kid had a nice little old lady to set up egg hunts, and knit them ugly socks. I had no grandmother, or even a grandfather for that matter. And that was that."

Lorrena closed her eyes, recalling memories of her younger years. She saw her father in his reading chair, telling her stories while she lay in bed. The words flew from the top of his head like doves beating their wings at any sudden disturbance. His tales went on without an end, until her eyes became so heavy his image would flick in and out of view. Falling into the darkness behind her eyelids, she'd hear his words grow further away. He whispered, "The gnomes...watching... over the hills they go...rolling in the creeks, catching trout in their teeth."

She remembered one particular night distinctly, when her eyes popped open to a misty shadow suspended above her father. It had transformed into a thin silhouette glistening in the dull light of her room. As she stared, it turned colors, each one of the rainbow, until she shut her eyes as tight as she could.

"Lorrena Bear, is everything okay?" her father had asked. But she couldn't remember answering. All that her memory revealed was the image of her father's face before she dozed off, his soft, subterranean brown eyes looking down on her. The warmth of his hand on her cheek.

The following day, her father was working at a house nearby when her family heard the news of a bad accident. A sudden slip from a ladder, her mother had said. Lorrena was only four. Not until years later, after her seventh birthday, did she begin to hear voices accompanying the images, like the mysterious shadow she had seen above her father. Now, although she couldn't touch them, the images were as real as the ground she walked on.

"If you can't feel them, they don't exist!" her mother insisted. But she had once proclaimed that Lorrena's grandmother no longer existed, either. The truth, although Lorrena couldn't hold it in her hands, was as clear as ever.

"Are you okay?" Ariel asked.

Lorrena blinked her eyes. "Yeah, just thinking." Pushing off of her left hand, she lifted herself up, trying to get a better view of the long driveway which extended from the left side of her house in a loop toward the road. The roar of an engine sounded. Soon after, the moving truck took off down the street, triggering Godiva's barking.

"Godiva, it's only the truck. Calm down," Lorrena said. She jogged over to her dog. Godiva was not facing the road, but toward the house.

"What is it, girl?" she asked, looking toward the windows. She held her hand above her eyes to shield them from oncoming snowflakes. Edna's figure settled in her mother's bedroom window. The wind rustled through the trees, accented by soft whispers. The voices resonated louder in her mind, so she closed her eyes tightly until they petered out.

"What is it?" Ariel asked.

"Oh, it's only Edna," Lorrena said, grabbing Godiva's collar as her barking subsided. "Let's go. Since the truck left, for sure my mother is already impatient to leave."

Lorrena unlatched the fence, then they headed up the hill toward the front door.

"I can hear her already. 'Lorrena Shaw, you're one and a half seconds late. Where are your manners, young lady?'" Ariel mimicked a motherly voice. She let out a loud huff before breaking out in giggles. "Man, am I going to miss you."

"Tell me about it." Lorrena sighed. "I'm gonna have to make fun of my mother with my dog. How fun will that be? And who's going to sit with me at lunch and pick out cute guys? Who will listen to my ghost stories?"

"Well, you've always got your new grandmother. You never know what she'll bring to the table."

"True." Lorrena lowered her bottom lip, forming the sad face they had often used to beg their parents for ice cream. "I'll sure miss you, Mermaid!"

"You too, Ghostbuster." Ariel squeezed her friend in a bear hug. "That's from Bob, too. He said he will always be your second dad, even if you're seven thousand miles away."

"Only like a hundred. Gloucester, Massachusetts. Wherever that may be." Lorrena shrugged.

"Even better. I'll see you later. Call my cell phone anytime!" Ariel yelled as she jogged down the driveway, the dog releasing a few barks as she departed.

"Let's go, girl. It's certainly a cold one today." Lorrena

hustled to the door trembling as Godiva followed her. The snow pressed down harder from the sky; a thin coating collected on the ground.

Lorrena ducked inside quickly. The house was eerily silent, the only noise coming from the shuffle of Lorrena's feet and the click of the dog's nails against the wood floor. Lorrena stopped in her tracks, waiting to hear anything aside from their own movement.

"Mom? Are you in here?" she called out. But there was no answer. As Lorrena rounded the corner, she found her mother sitting on a box facing the window. Her hands were folded in her lap. Above her, a soft white glow twinkled. Lorrena held her gaze on the light form, mesmerized as it grew brighter. It took the muffled shape of her father's face before reaching a point of absolute intensity. Abruptly, it burnt out.

"Mom, are you okay? I've been calling you," Lorrena said, releasing more concern in her tone than she had expected.

"Oh yeah. Sorry, Lorrena," Erin said. Without turning around she rose quickly to her feet. She smoothed her hair and ran her hands under her eyes before she spun to face her daughter. "The movers couldn't fit this last box. Let's go load it into the car and hit the road."

Lorrena nodded, detecting a glassy ball of water welling up in the corner of her mother's eye. Erin flicked it away with one flick of her finger and everything from then on moved in slow motion, as if Lorrena was locked in a daydream ensuing with every blink.

Her arms swung back and forth as she walked past the empty bookcases, toward her mother standing with her head dipped down. In reverse, Lorrena moved backward through the hallway, her arms as light as feathers, the box like a bird flying weightless through the air. The windows displayed a view of the snow filled sky. She took a quick right-hand glimpse of the kitchen, her father's hard work carved into the cabinets, empty, and out the door they went, with Godiva following at their feet.

The snowflakes dissolved on Lorrena's nose as they shuffled toward the car. The windshield was covered with snow. Securing the box in the trunk, Lorrena found the scraper to knock off the snow that caked the windows. Her hands tensed as the flakes hit her bare skin.

After the car was cleaned, Lorrena tucked herself beside Godiva in the backseat of their red Ford Focus. She rubbed her hands together, the idle engine singing as they waited for the car to gain warmth. Her mother stared off into the distance in a dreamlike hush. Not a word was spoken when they finally took off down the driveway.

Lorrena observed in the mirror her childhood as it disappeared out of view. They drove down the roads Lorrena often claimed she could walk with her eyes closed. Past the local post office where her mother sent her to mail letters. Past the church where she had been baptized many years before quitting her weekly attendance. The town beach where she and Ariel learned to swim. It all whirled by her, left behind.

The wipers darted across the windshield, shoving the snow aside. Keeping one hand on Godiva's back, Lorrena saw the familiar sights transform into the highway, leading them to a place she attempted to picture in her mind, but couldn't.

Without warning, her mother cleared her throat. "We moved to that house almost twenty-five years ago, your father and I," she said.

Lorrena nearly jumped when her mother interrupted her thoughts.

Erin continued without hesitation. "It was a mess then.

Your father wanted it that way, because we got it for a good price. He wanted to fix it up to make it our own, even though he knew it was a tough job. But the more difficult something was, the harder your father tried to perfect it." She paused, taking one hand off the steering wheel to wipe her eyes. "It took nearly a year to get that place livable. We worked long, fast hours. It had been torn up from a fire."

"Wow," was all Lorrena could say. She remembered immediately Edna's constant talk about tending to the fire.

"Did anyone die in it?" she asked.

"Oh, I don't know," her mother answered with irritation. "You expect me to know everything?"

Lorrena felt the urge to yell out that yes, she did expect it. That there was so much her mother was keeping from her. Rather than making a scene, she remained quiet, knowing full well that her mother did and said what she wanted, without anyone telling her otherwise. She waited for her mother to continue, but Erin said nothing more.

Curious, Lorrena took out her cell phone and searched the Internet for "Bobby's death in a fire" along with her address. To her surprise, many articles popped up, revealing that a woman named Suzanne Morris had died after the house went up in a blaze. Her son, Robert, also known as Bobby, had apparently left the door to the woodstove open by accident, allowing kindling beside the woodstove to catch fire, and then the kitchen table, until most of the house went up. His mother was a charismatic yet stubborn woman who rarely left her home. She couldn't get out in time, and was survived by her son, Bobby Morris, and her husband, Elliot Morris, who had been out fishing that day with his crew. Lorrena laughed quietly to herself that she had been referring to Suzanne as Edna all this time.

One of the articles, dated five years after the fire had taken place, indicated that nobody had been brave enough to buy the house and rebuild it, until a young couple took on the project. *My parents*, she realized. Lorrena couldn't believe that even the article claimed the place might be haunted.

If they only knew, Lorrena thought.

She read through each of the articles, amazed that her mother had failed to let her know what had happened. Soon after, Lorrena felt a rush of exhaustion wash over her due to the previous nights' lack of sleep. The lull of the wipers, the cars passing by, and a soft murmuring of voices filled her ears. She closed her eyes for what seemed like a few minutes.

When she opened them the car was turning through an awkward intersection, rolling to a stop into a gravel driveway directly off to the right. Godiva nudged her shoulder, stepping onto her lap to lick her face.

"Where are we, Godey? Are we here already?" Lorrena asked, lifting Godiva back onto the seat so she could get out.

Her mother had already left the vehicle, making her way across the snowy lawn. "We're here," she said, looking up at the house with her arms crossed.

The house was small with five windows surrounding a thick oak door. In the middle was a doorknocker in the shape of a lion. The outside walls consisted of dark wooden shingles. The driveway extended behind the house, hugging one side of a cemetery enclosed by a black fence that wound up to the right, disappearing over a hill covered in trees. Lorrena heard the commotion of the movers who were unloading boxes at the back of the house.

"This is it, Lorrena. My own childhood home. Can you believe it?" Erin's tone was laced with both enthusiasm and apprehension.

Lorrena stood in shock. "Are you kidding?" She looked up at the structure, her mouth gaping open. The house was nothing to brag about. The shingles were faded in spots, and a crack cut across one window. But there was an antique air about it that intrigued her. The stained glass window above the door was half-moon shaped, marked by dividers which moved inwards toward the center.

"So, does this mean my grandmother is inside waiting for us?" Lorrena cried out, unable to hide her excitement.

Her mother's response was heated. "No," she said as she headed across the grass to unlock the door. With a loud creaking of the door's hinges, she disappeared into their new home.

CHAPTER FIVE

Patricia Pollaski

Wednesday -- February 25th -- 6:38 p.m.

“Time for dinner, Mrs. Reynolds,” Patricia said, placing the woman's folded shirts into two precise piles on her bed.

The woman appeared to be looking straight at her. Deep blue veins scrawled across her bony hands, clutching her wheelchair. Yet her eyes displayed a vacancy common in many of the residents at Kendall Retirement. In some cases, they would not respond for hours, as if they temporarily checked out of their bodies, returning again at random moments. Opening the door to their blank stare, the substance of personality would reemerge, their senses keen and alert again.

Many times during her first week back to work, Patricia closed her eyes for a few moments too, trying to learn the secrets of their escape. The distant buzz of the television suspended in her ears, and the potent smell of rubbing alcohol creeping up around her reminded her that she was still there, stuck within the confines of her mind.

Patricia blinked. Looking deep into the emptiness of the woman's pale blue irises, she assumed that perhaps the woman was listening and only needed something happy and familiar to bring her back into reality.

"Turkey cutlets, mashed potatoes, and green beans tonight. Your favorite," Patricia said as she patted the woman's soft white sweater. "Ahhh, but I guess I'll have to eat it for you if you're going to sit and daydream." Patricia picked up the remote, switching off the Gold Bond advertisement. "What about that pumpkin pie too? Whipped cream melted on top. Mmm, mmm good."

Evidence of a weary smile touched the corners of the woman's mouth, but she didn't answer.

Flicking off the light, Patricia rolled the wheelchair backward through the doorway and down the long hall so that Mrs. Reynolds' feet did not get stuck underneath the chair. Patricia's sneakers were silent against the gray carpet as she pushed. Many of the other residents were already in the dining room, adding to the hush of the empty halls. As she walked, Patricia admired the paintings of the ocean scenes scattered between the doorways—rocks along the beach's edge drenched in sea spray; waves reaching up and over the sides of sailboats as they bounced across the Gloucester Harbor.

As the lady began to speak, Patricia turned her attention to the fluffy gray hair sticking up from her head.

"I need to pick my son up from school today," Mrs. Reynolds said, her words wavering. "I need to take him to his piano lessons."

"Don't worry about it, Mrs. Reynolds. Everything is taken

care of," Patricia replied. The words repeated in her head, a dull ache resurfacing in her chest. *My son.*

Patricia tapped the handicapped button, the doors springing to life. Holding the door open with her left hand as they passed through, she directed the wheelchair toward the dining room on the right side of the lobby. Many of the men and women were already eating. Some were being hand-fed, while others lifted their wobbly arms gradually with forks full of food.

"But I promised him I'd bring cookies. I have to go, I have to leave now," the old woman said.

"It's okay, Mrs. Reynolds. Look, there's Mrs. Franklin. How about we have dinner with her tonight?"

"Yeah," she said, pausing. "I'd like that."

Patricia pushed her over to the free space at the table, yanking the chair aside. The dining room consisted of four long tables covered in lacy red tablecloths marked with chairs, which were moved for the residents with wheelchairs.

"Patricia, Mrs. Reynolds, so glad you could join us this evening," Mrs. Marietta said. She walked toward them with a plate of food.

As the director of the retirement home, Mrs. Marietta often kept watch over the entire scene, and was not specifically assigned to the rooms as Patricia was before she'd taken time off. Since Patricia's return the previous Monday, she had decided to keep her assignments minimal until she regained complete composure.

"We got a little caught up in watching 'The Three Stooges,' but we made it," Patricia said, unfolding a cloth napkin and spreading it across the old woman's lap.

Mrs. Marietta placed the plate down on the table. "There you go, Mrs. Reynolds."

The lady didn't acknowledge them. Staring down at her food, she called out, "Where is my son? I want to see my son!"

Patricia stroked the woman's shoulder. "It's time to eat your dinner now, Mrs. Reynolds. Your son was in to visit yesterday. He'll be back soon, don't worry," she said in her most comforting voice. The old woman's son would be back to visit her the next week, and the week after that, maybe even a few times, Patricia wanted to say. And he would see her, alive, slightly inattentive, murmuring something about how the sun was shining so fierce that day.

"I'm going to be *late*," Mrs. Reynolds muttered under her breath.

"Look, Mrs. Reynolds, it's dark outside now. It's time for dinner." Patricia pointed out the window. The blue sheer curtains hung around the corners of the window, accentuating the snow glistening across the walkway in the dim light of the lampposts. She remembered a time many years ago when she could see from the very same window her husband escorting their children to the lobby. There they would talk to the residents while he went off to his meeting. Another time, her son had left school early feeling sick, and hiked down the walkway with his head lowered, his face flushed. Patricia's son would never be back to see her in the nursing home.

"Oh, I love dinnertime," Mrs. Reynolds said.

Grabbing a fork, Patricia scooped up a mound of mashed potatoes. "Here, I'll help you with your first few mouthfuls, and then you can take over."

Mrs. Reynolds allowed Patricia to spoon the potatoes past her chapped lips before taking the responsibility into her own hands. The turkey cutlets had been pureed into mounds of brown mush, the green beans mixed among them like grass growing from dirt piles. Slowly and steadily, she consumed her meal with a few mumbles in between bites.

Patricia looked around at the wrinkled faces, lit by gleaming lights hanging down over their heads. The aroma of the night's meal blended with the strong scent of the pine tree they had set up for the holidays. Simple white lights encircled the tree Patricia's husband had cut down, which they'd kept barely alive with a trash can top full of water. Lights followed around the corners of the ceiling and up over the fireplace. Mrs. Marietta had also taped cardboard snowflakes around the walls.

"Patricia, how are you doing?" she heard someone say from behind her.

Patricia turned to find an attendant by the name of Jean, her acquaintance since she had started working at the home a few years after her son was born.

"I'm getting by," Patricia answered with a slight hesitation. She heard her words being spoken at a distance, as if coming from someone else. "I mean, what else can I do, you know? I can't stop. I just keep moving, no matter how hard it is." She fiddled with a napkin without meeting the woman's eyes.

"I'm so sorry about your loss," Jean said with a nervous sigh. "Man, it's so difficult to know what to say in these situations. I guess I just wanted you to know that if you needed anything, Rob and I are here. Christopher sends his condolences, too."

Finally looking up at Jean, Patricia recalled times their children had spent together in the lobby waiting for them to leave work. She saw them making faces at the residents through the fish tank on the snowy afternoons when school was cancelled. Pushing the images out of her mind, Patricia released her words without thinking. "Thank you. We've gotten a lot of support from family and friends, and we're very appreciative. It's strange, though. As grateful as I am to have so many kind thoughts, no matter how many people I have around for support, it's like…the only person I really want to see isn't here. I keep thinking he'll call me tomorrow, but I have to remind myself it won't happen. He's not alive any-more." Patricia let the napkin fall from her hands. "And then I look around at all of these people in the nursing home who've made it so long. Why not him? Why couldn't he be here some day?"

"Yeah, I don't know, Patty," Jean said, helping Mr. Enid catch the last green bean onto his fork. "That's what's so crazy about life. No one really has an answer to that."

"Well, why not? Why can't we know?"

Jean shrugged without answering.

Patricia stopped moving and watched the snow fall from the tree branches. "I don't know what to believe anymore."

"Well, can you believe it's almost the end of February? I sure can't," Jean said. "Doesn't it feel like a few days ago that summer was ending?"

"Yeah, time's been flying. I can't get a handle on it," Patricia replied. She picked up the napkin beside Mrs. Reynolds hands and wiped remnants of her meal from her upper lip.

"That's what happens when you're old. Time disinte-grates like your teeth," a woman said from across the table. Mrs. Gedolewen, one of the new residents, smiled at Patricia from her wheelchair. She was a small woman, her scrawny shoulders fastened into a hunched position. Her hair was rolled into tight gray curls which hung just above her brown plaid sweater and the folds of skin dangling from her neck. Resting on the end of her pointy nose was a pair of oval glasses, her blue eyes peering out through the miniature lenses.

"I'll take your pumpkin pie then," said Mr. Harl. "I lost

mine years ago. Ever since, I been eatin' enough sugar to fill two bathtubs!" He laughed, making sure to show the shiny white dentures molded to his mouth.

"Oh, quit your bragging. Diabetes will catch up to you any day now," Mrs. Franklin said. She stood to shift her chair, showing off her mobility.

"Not for a little while at least," Mrs. Gedolewen mumbled. "Patricia, would you mind taking me back to my room? I think I'd like to sit and watch some television. You know, relax a little bit. Rest the legs." With a raised eyebrow, the old woman pointed to her feet, which Patricia knew were propped up on the wheelchair's metal footrest hidden beneath the table.

"Sure thing, Mrs. Gedolewen."

"Oh, please. Call me Miriam. It makes me sound so much younger. I keep telling my husband every day I'm dropping that name, anyway. No one knows how to spell the damn thing! Not like my eyes are working anymore, but for goodness' sake, I'm surprised I can still get my voice going after making so many corrections. Guh-*dole*-win. But no, the name is Miriam."

"Well it certainly is a toughie if you don't know exactly how to say it." Patricia tossed Mrs. Reynold's dirty napkin onto her plate.

"Jean, would you mind taking over Mrs. Reynolds' care for the evening while I bring Miriam to her room?"

"Sure, Patricia."

"Thanks," Patricia said, making her way to Mrs. Gedolewen's side. She pulled back the handles of the wheelchair to release it from under the table. "Miriam is a nice name, but don't you think your husband will be sad if you get rid of the other part?"

"Oh, he's not alive anymore. He won't mind," the old

woman said as she swept her brittle hand across the air. "By golly, I don't think he'd care even if he was. He was a simple sort of guy."

Patricia maneuvered the wheelchair through the narrow aisle between the tables, following behind the men and women exiting the dining room in clusters. Into the lobby they progressed, like snails appearing not to move, yet covering ground in a sly, drawn-out motion.

"I see," Patricia said, stopping as the woman in front of her casually tapped the handicapped button with the end of her cane. "Do you have any children? What would they think about it?"

Mrs. Gedolewen chuckled. "I'm so old, I don't even remember if I do! You'd think I'd recall something as important as that, hmm?" The creases of her face folded inward as she smiled. "The truth is, it's been about twenty-five years since I've seen my daughter."

"I see," Patricia said, sucking in a gasp. She squinted to fight back the tears. If this woman's child had died, she didn't want to know about it. "Oh look, here we are at your room. Number 17, right? Is the woman who shares your room back from dinner yet? I don't remember seeing her."

"Doris checked out a few weeks ago, on a Wednesday," Mrs. Gedolewen said casually. "Passed away in her sleep."

Tension surged through Patricia's arms. She cursed to herself for acting so absentminded. She remembered the director telling her of Doris Freedman's passing when she had picked up her new pairs of scrubs on her first day back to work. She recognized the importance of comforting the folks at the nursing home during situations like these. As their friends went missing one by one, each employee supported the memorial of the departed, while keeping the hype at a minimum so the residents wouldn't go into states of shock—if they were not there already.

Patricia tapped on the lights, revealing the room exactly as she remembered it two days before. Mrs. Gedolewen's side of the room, closest to the window, contained a bed covered in blue hospital blankets and a dresser with a single picture frame on top, the size of a teacup. Beside it was a bouquet of plastic daisies housed within a white vase. Doris's bed had been completely stripped of sheets, but beside it were a bunch of white roses remaining there in her memory. The flowers were touched by fatality, their white petals browning at the edges.

"I'm sorry. It slipped my mind. I've been so distracted lately, I can barely differentiate yesterday from today," Patricia said.

"It's okay," Mrs. Gedolewen said. "Everything will be okay."

Patricia noticed a glint of nostalgia in the old woman's eyes, the way her brows perked up above a stare so sharp she feared it strong enough to shatter the window. It was not a harsh look, not angry or melancholy, but one that had been built up over years of survival.

"I don't know that it will." Patricia felt her ability to suppress her insistent feelings of dejection slip out from under her.

Mrs. Gedolewen raised her chin up, the focus of her stare untraceable. "Our paths in life are no highway. Now and again, we all think we're speeding along fine, the wind catching our hair, hitting our face with a warm careening gesture. Then, boom! We realize we're going the wrong way or we blink our eyes and suddenly we're driving down a road laced with pebbles, with one big boulder in the way. No matter our tight grip on reality, we begin to feel absolutely powerless. We recognize there's nothing we can do but turn around and keep moving. We go and go, and maybe we pause once in a while, but we never stop growing. And in that sense, we are more powerful than we often recognize."

Patricia listened to the hum of the fluorescent lights in the silence that followed. The old woman's speech repeated in her mind.

"I guess I just don't understand the purpose of anything, if life is there and then gone in such a small period of—"

"Time...which only appears to be slipping," Mrs. Gedolewen said softly as if it were a secret no one else could know.

"Slipping," Patricia repeated, pushing the wheelchair into the bathroom to prepare the old woman for sleep. As she assisted Mrs. Gedolewen in changing into her gown, brushing her teeth and then helping her into bed, she was reminded of circumstances years ago, when she was the mother of a little boy. She remembered her son's Superman pajamas, his red toothbrush. The way he wiped the excess toothpaste from his mouth with his sleeve, bounding into his racecar bed under Superman sheets he pulled up to his nose. He would shut his eyes tight, wishing for sleep. Where had the Jimmy of these scenes gone? Memories existed, so fragile and elusive, before reality pushed them away.

Patricia tucked the blanket over the woman's arms. She lay on her back, her head swallowed by the white feather pillow.

"I've been trying so hard, but I just can't stay awake any longer. Will you tell her that I'm going to sleep now?" Mrs. Gedolewen whispered, her eyelids flickering to a close.

"Tell who, Miriam?" Patricia asked, but the old woman mumbled something she couldn't decipher.

"Goodnight," Patricia murmured. "Sweet dreams."

She tiptoed across the linoleum floor. As she flipped the light switch, the room became immersed in moonlight. She headed out the door, closing it carefully with a quiet click.

Patricia released a sigh of relief, relaxing her shoulders. Finally, she could go home and rest her aching body, enjoy the feeling of stillness. Approaching the lobby, she came upon Mrs. Marietta pushing a cart stacked with clean laundry bins.

"Oh, good," Mrs. Marietta said. "Just the woman I wanted to see. Before you go home tonight, would you mind folding the laundry and preparing for tomorrow? It won't take long, I promise."

Patricia forced a smile. "Sure," she said through her teeth. Anxiety slipped back into her chest, worries filling her cranium. *What is the point of clean laundry when it just gets dirty again and again? What is the point of anything? It's all just a tiresome never-ending cycle.*

"Thanks so much." Mrs. Marietta hurried to the door. "I've got to take care of some things."

Patricia picked up the fabric, warm against her fingertips. Folding napkins, pillowcases, sheets, and scrubs, she situated them into stacks, counting them one by one to pass the time. Digging into the endless bin of fresh laundry, she heard the bell signal. Glancing at her watch, the numerals read sixteen past nine. Nearly fifteen minutes had gone by, neither swift nor sluggish. *Another blurring of moments loaded with his reflection. Time slipping away*, she thought.

As the door swung open, a girl in her mid-teens stepped into the lobby, her parka damp from the freshly fallen snow. Frizzy brown hair stuck out from her woolen hat.

"Hi," the girl said.

"Hello, may I help you?"

"Yes. I've come to see Mrs. Miriam Gedolewen."

Patricia hesitated, but then thought otherwise of allowing the girl into the room. "I'm sorry, visiting hours ended an hour ago. She's sleeping now, but you could come back in the morning?"

The girl's expression displayed panic, her eyes widening as she glared at Patricia. "Um, sure. I guess I will. Thank you."

"Would you like me to take your—"

Before Patricia could finish her sentence, the girl was out the door, the bell chiming its mellow tune as she left.

CHAPTER
SIX

Lorrena Shaw

Wednesday -- February 25th -- 9:18 p.m.

As a translucent figure emerged over the nursing home attendant's head, Lorrena's pulse quickened, her heart soaring up into her throat. Her arms prickled with goose bumps. The image transformed into a young man whose skin shone with dazzling luminosity, growing brighter the more Lorrena focused. His eyes burned a deep blue. In a split second, his hand descended over the woman's blonde hair, his other hand pressed against his chest.

The woman didn't flinch. "I'm sorry, visiting hours ended an hour ago. She's sleeping now, but you could come back in the morning?"

Lorrena's chin dropped, her eyes fixed on the guy until he disappeared in a swirling cloud. The air was clear once more.

"Um, sure. I guess I will. Thank you," she said. Dashing

out the door, the roar of the wind blurred the woman's response.

Lorrena's legs carried her down the walkway, a chilling blast of air pinching her cheeks. She couldn't get the picture out of her mind. The insightful look on the young man's face, the clear representation of his body. It was unlike anything she had seen before. Typically manifesting before Lorrena's eyes were lost souls who wandered the planet, ignoring peoples' presences completely. The energy forces that spoke to her directly did not usually materialize into any apparent form, like her father's representation, which had never been as definitive as the random ghosts she caught lurking around.

Lorrena released an angry sigh. She had not even gotten to see her grandmother. She was beginning to think that the woman did not exist. Cringing at the thought of the long walk back to her house, she wondered if her mother had even noticed that she'd left earlier that evening. Lorrena had bombarded Erin with so many questions about her grandmother's whereabouts that her mother finally muttered the direction of the nursing home down the street. Buried deep in her unpacking project, Erin was probably too busy to notice she had snuck out the back door. Lorrena hoped she could tiptoe upstairs, back into bed with her warm blankets, without her mother suspecting anything.

The ice crusted on the sidewalk crunched beneath her sneakers. Hugging her upper body as she walked, Lorrena counted the steps that led her closer to her new home. *Fifteen, sixteen, seventeen.*

Lorrena froze when she heard a car slow down behind her. She turned, squinting as the headlights shone in her eyes. The car pulled over to the sidewalk. Lorrena read the words *Gloucester Police* scrawled across the doors.

"Excuse me, Miss? What are you up to this chilly evening?" the policeman asked after getting out of the car. He held up his immense black flashlight. "I'm just concerned for your safety. It's a little cold and dark for a young person like you to be going for a walk, don't you think?"

"I'm on my way home," Lorrena said.

"May I ask your name and birth date please?" he said in a deeper voice.

"Lorrena Shaw, April Eighth..." Her body quivered.

Tucking the flashlight under his arm, he pulled out a mini leather notebook and began scribbling. Shifting his gaze in Lorrena's direction, the policeman hesitated. "I'd offer you a ride home, but it's actually against our policy and procedure without your parents' permission. Why don't we give them a call?" He waved his free arm toward the car. "First, let's check to see if you've been reported missing. You can hop in the backseat for now."

Lorrena bit her lip. The handle made a snapping sound as he pulled open the door, tiny ice pieces scattering onto the street. Although Lorrena worried about her mother's scolding, her apprehension quickly turned to anger. There was nothing for her mother to complain about. It was Erin's fault for not taking Lorrena to the nursing home right away. Lorrena's only option was to trek out into the dark night to seal the void in her mind.

Lorrena faltered as she unsuccessfully attempted to squeeze into the police car.

"There you are, almost. Sit down first, and then swing your legs in," the policeman said. He closed the door behind her after she awkwardly pushed herself into the seat behind the metal screen. Through the plexi-glass, she watched the officer getting into the driver's seat.

He typed into a computer. "Your parents number, please?"

Lorrena blurted out her mother's cell phone number, tensing as she spoke each number aloud. If her mother grounded her, she would never get to see her grandmother.

Leaning her head against the glass, Lorrena heard distant ringing from the device. "Yes, Mrs. Shaw? This is Officer Draydon with the Gloucester Police. Not to worry, but I have your daughter with me. Is it okay if I bring her by in my car?"

Lorrena heard her mother's shrill reply.

"Yes, ma'am, she's all right. We'll be right there." There was a loud click. Static buzzed briefly before dying out.

Lorrena kept her mouth shut. She watched the cemetery pass by. As they approached her house, Erin's head peeked out from behind the door.

"Lorrena! What the hell do you think you're doing?"

The policeman opened the door for Lorrena to climb out of the car, escorting her to the steps. Her mother's voice cracked. "I'm so sorry, Officer. Are you sure everything is okay? I don't know what's gotten into her."

"I assure you, everything is fine, ma'am," he said with a nod.

"Calm down, Mother," Lorrena said. "I went to visit my grandmother because *you* wouldn't take me. This nice policeman here stopped to give me a ride home."

"Thank you so much," Erin said. Her trite smile transformed into a grimace as she looked toward her daughter. "Lorrena, come here." She pointed her finger at the front steps.

"Oh, c'mon. I'm not your dog," Lorrena said. The policeman had already walked back to his car as Lorrena slowly ambled up the cement steps, stopping in front of her mother.

"I'm your mother and I can talk to you however I please."

Godiva poked her nose out from behind Erin's hip. Barking, the dog bolted across the driveway, nudging through a broken tier in the fence. She took off across the graveyard, her brown body appearing as a dark speck against the white snow.

"Godiva, come back!" Lorrena called, running after her. She hopped over the top of the fence, dodging the headstones. The trees' thick, bare branches overhead hung high above the stones like a canopy, shedding clumps of snow when the wind blew. As she sprinted in her dog's footprints, Lorrena kicked up cold slush into her pant legs.

"Here, Godey! Here girl!" Lorrena yelled, but all she could see were the tracks leading behind rows of headstones extending over the hill. Numerous tree trunks dotting the graveyard prevented a clear view of the space around her. Lorrena stopped to catch her breath, her chest stinging as she sucked in gulps of air. She listened to the sound of her wheezing as oxygen struggled to pass through her body.

Besides her commotion, the graveyard was surprisingly silent. Godiva had stopped barking. The sudden stillness propelled tremors up her back and into her ears, stopping her midstep. She waited for a lost poltergeist the color of icicles to pop out from behind a tombstone, filling her ears with loud cries. But there was nothing. Not a bark, not even the creaking of branches.

No sooner had the thought crossed her mind, Lorrena's shoulders pressed back in distress. A soft breeze drifted through the trees, boughs bending as the light current grew into a stronger blast of air which yanked her hair across her face. Lorrena winced, her skin tender from the unrelenting winter atmosphere.

"What the—" she mumbled, the question frozen at her lips.

Lorrena watched as more snow fell onto the gravestone in front of her. Snowflakes glistened in a sliver of moonlight, allowing her to scan the lines etched into the granite. The stone was small and curved around the top. It read: "James David," with snow covering his last name and his birth date. He had died only a few weeks ago, on February 3rd. The words centered on the bottom of the grave, sheltered from the weather, were carved in script: *Reaching the end of his days at too young an age, our loving son will live in our hearts, always.*

Lorrena again raised her chin toward the sky, the cold air finding its way through her scarf onto her bare neck. The clouds had nearly disintegrated, uncovering stars speckled over the dark blanket of night.

The echo of Godiva's barking rang out once again. For a moment, she had forgotten why she was roaming around in the cemetery without a flashlight to begin with. *You're crazy, Lorrena*, she told herself. But the panic associated with wandering atop the resting places of the dead still had not set in. There was nothing here to fear but the darkness, and the absence of her dog whose bark turned on and off like the television sometimes did when Lorrena sat in front of it. It was beyond her power. The idea that her mother had not come out to retrieve her sent a rush of worry through her body.

To her relief, the howling sounded closer. Listening attentively, she noticed a sound she couldn't quite pinpoint, resonating through her dog's whine. Had the voices returned? "Godiva, where are you, girl?" Lorrena called, her throat burning.

Scurrying around a broad oak tree, Lorrena noticed a memorial built into the hill, its metal door slightly open. Meandering over the tombs was one thing, but to go inside of a tomb was a task she didn't think she could undertake. Lorrena treaded softly toward the door, peering into the shadows. The eerie murmur intensified, and for a moment she believed it to be a voice asking who was intruding.

"Godey, are you in there?" Lorrena asked, but as she stood up straight, the tree branches shook. She discovered the sounds were not coming from in the tomb or in her head, but high up in the tree. The figure of a small owl perched on a branch could be seen as she hiked up the hill. Godiva sat below it, mesmerized by the owl. Its yellow eyes pierced the darkness, and as it let out its call, the dog answered back with a nervous bark.

"It's okay, Godey. It's just a little owl. Nothing to be afraid of," Lorrena said. The owl's feathers shook like the bird had the chills, too. A strange feeling came over her as it stared back, calling, "Whooo, whooo."

"Who?" Lorrena repeated.

With a sudden swoop onto the gravestone, the owl again ruffled its feathers. Lifting its head toward the heavens, it flew off into the night.

Lorrena trembled, taking hold of Godiva by her collar. "It's time to go back home now," she said, dragging the dog toward the fence. Snow crept further into her socks, leaving her toes fully numb. As they got closer, she heard Erin's muffled calls from the doorway. "Lorrena!"

"Yeah, Mom, we're coming," Lorrena said as she finally reached the front steps.

"Lorrena, there you are! What the hell took you so long? I've been calling you this entire time! Why haven't you answered me?"

"I couldn't hear you. I was way over the hill looking for Godiva and I couldn't find her." Lorrena darted by her mother, into the house. Warmth radiated from the fireplace, and her body stung all over. She removed her jacket and sweater, boots and socks before collapsing into the faded green armchair that smelled of soot and mothballs. They had brought all of their furniture to storage, the boxes filled with their daily necessities dropped into the back of the house. The miniscule living room was still filled with her grandmother's antique couches and chairs. There was a box packed with trinkets like silver candleholders, tall brown candles, and black-and-white photos of people she didn't recognize.

"I was worried sick about you, damnit. Why do you have to take off like that?" Her mother's hands rested on her hips. "This just—it isn't right. I'm going to start handing out consequences if you're going to pull any more stupid runaway stunts."

"You couldn't drive me to the nursing home, or come find me when the dog ran away? It's not like there were any ghosts out there. It was actually pretty calm. It really is true when they say that their bodies rest in peacefulness. It's only when their spirits are running around that they make lots of noise."

Erin sighed in annoyance. "Lorrena, it is not about the silly things you think you see with your eyes. What about the dangerous things that you could actually encounter, like a kidnapper or a rabid animal? You can't just run around wherever you damn well please, especially in places you don't know."

"Well, it's not like you were going to take me to see my grandmother anyway. What's up with that? Why don't you want to see your own mother? I mean, I have to every day."

"Lorrena, don't get smart with me."

"But I feel like I know nothing, Mom. We came here to take care of her, and we haven't even seen her yet." Lorrena's words were coated with frustration.

Erin nodded her head, flustered. "I just haven't had the

time. This moving has got me running around everywhere."

"Right. Everywhere except the one place you should be. For all I know, my grandmother could be sick in bed, dying in her sleep. Then I'll never get to see her except floating around our new house. When did you two live here, anyway? Why don't I know what's going on? Do you think that's right, keeping your daughter away from her family after all of these years?" Lorrena stood, infuriated.

Her mother didn't answer. She paced a few steps back and forth before stiffly releasing her words, which hung like the smoke in the air:

"I ran away," Erin said. "I ran away twenty some odd years ago, and no, I have not seen my mother for any of that time, not even once. Is that enlightening enough for you? Is that what you want to know? I—I—" she stuttered. "I have to sleep now. We'll talk about this tomorrow, after your first day of school. Good night, Lorrena." Erin turned to walk up the wooden staircase lining the wall.

Lorrena's mouth dropped. She could hardly believe her ears. "You what? How—how could you do such a thing? After all of those times you scolded me for running away and you were the one who needed the scolding!"

"Lorrena, enough. To bed, now."

"But we need to talk about this, Mom. How could you go twenty years without even a word? It's just not fair, to me or to your own mom!"

"Life isn't fair, Lorrena. Let it go. It's late, and you have a busy day ahead of you. Get some sleep."

"But I feel like this is never going to happen. If we don't talk about it, it will disappear. She'll remain a figment of my imagination, an eerie image like all of the other ghosts I see."

"Cut your nonsense. We'll talk about it tomorrow, and

that's final."

Disappointment flooded through Lorrena's body as she stumbled toward the stairs. The floor was warm against her bare feet, but she did not feel settled. Her head ached, the voices pushing through her skull. Whenever she lost control of her emotions, the voices became harder to restrain. The floorboards creaked as her mother ascended the staircase. *Rest*, one voice urged. Lorrena cupped her hands over her ears as if to keep the sounds from entering, but the clutter of words persisted. Another part of her mind begged for answers. She was so close to the truth, yet she knew her mother's tendency to hold firm to her declarations.

A wave of exhaustion swept over Lorrena. "I am pretty tired," she said. Her mother turned left down the slender hallway as Lorrena ducked in the other direction toward her new bedroom. Erin's room was directly parallel to hers.

"I'll wake you up by six o'clock, Lorrena. Sleep well," Erin said. She closed the door softly, her blank look disappearing behind the wooden panels.

Turning on her lamp, Lorrena looked around her room. She took a long breath in and out through her nose. The floors were still covered in boxes. Her bed was tucked into the corner, the sheets thrown on so that the left edge of the mattress popped out. The air smelled musty, the windows hidden behind thick shutters with flowers drawn around them.

Lorrena jumped into her bed, pulling the covers up to her waist. Questions raced through her mind. Taking her journal out from under her pillow, she scribbled her thoughts down on paper: her mother's possible motives for running away; a new day filled with introductions to new high school students who were so quick to judge; the never-ending pages of schoolwork, which would soon occupy her precious time. She counted the hours that would have to pass until she could finally see her grandmother. After Lorrena's hand grew tired, she tucked her journal into the backpack beside her bed.

"Just fall asleep, Lorrena," she said to herself. "Stop thinking."

Time moved so much faster during sleep. But now, her thoughts were easy to sustain. It seemed effortless for her mother to keep the old woman away. Perhaps her grandmother had been an awful person. Maybe her mother was protecting her from someone not even worth knowing.

Rest, the voices whispered again.

Colors formed behind her eyes as she slipped further into slumber. Reds swirling into blacks, blending into blotchy yellow patches. She moved deeper into dreams she kept hidden away within the crevices of her memory, awakened only when she reached the point where her unconscious mind took over.

She was flying. The kind of flight where she was one moment in her bed, falling asleep, and the next moment she was outside of herself, watching her hands cradle the left side her face. Her knees were tucked into a tight ball, chest moving up and down beneath fleece blankets. She now hovered above this sleeping girl, free.

A man appeared at her side. "Come this way, Lorrena. We have so much to see this night." He waved her toward the ceiling.

The man was dressed in all white, she thought, but then his entire being shifted colors so she couldn't quite pinpoint the details. He looked like the spirits she saw in her waking state. For now, she too had become like them. Her body glimmered as she followed him through the wall into a star-filled sky.

They flew, not up, but through the layers of the stars into

a light that was so oddly bright it did not hurt her eyes. As they entered into the brilliant hole together, it was as if her—the man—the entire world—became one.

The man was James, she knew. She often spent time with him soaring through the stratosphere to a place she remembered only when their astral bodies returned. An alternative dimension, Home to those who spoke in the hushed words Lorrena could not fully understand.

Suddenly, the sky transformed into an immense room with white pillars holding up the ceiling so high above her, she could not find their limits. The floors were made of the purest ivory tiles. Spiral staircases wound upward, making Lorrena dizzy as she followed them with her eyes. There were several other people around them, floating across the tile like they no longer needed their feet. Lorrena glided the same way, a force unexpectedly pulling her toward enormous white doors with roses etched into their frame.

The doors opened as they approached.

Millions of bookcases filled with thick books were set up around the walls. Lorrena's eyes darted in all directions, the shelves wrapping around endless corners. No matter how hard she tried, she could find no boundaries to the rooms surrounding them. It was as if her notion of distance had dislodged itself. Time and space were obsolete.

"We'll make this easier for you," James said, placing his hands together, palm to palm. As he pulled apart his thumbs to make an imaginary book, real pages formed within his hands, and through his skin emerged its binding.

"I don't understand," she said. "Is this book for me?"

"It is my Life Book." His mouth contorted into a wry smile. "But it's for you to read, and understand. A part of my Records that correlates to yours."

James held out the book. As Lorrena clutched its soft red cover, instead of running her fingers through the pages bound within, she found no paper, no words. She felt herself slipping into the text, as if the only way to read it was to experience it.

The library faded into a cloudless sky. The smooth ivory floor became a road, her hands securing around metal handles. She was riding a motorcycle, bounding along the road at the edge of the clear, blue ocean.

Although she could not see him, James was still with her. His voice echoed around her, ringing in her ears.

"You remember my story. It was mine to write, and then to live out. Now I hand pieces of my story over to you."

The motorcycle flew across the opposite lane of the highway. Without warning, Lorrena's hands released the handlebars as forces beyond her control pulled her from the motorcycle and into the bottom of the cliff.

Her heart jumped, her body shaking. Her eyes burst open as she felt herself falling from the bed. But she wasn't falling at all. She had somehow wedged herself between the bed and the wall. Rubbing her eyes touched with the stickiness of sleep, she leaned backward to glare at the clock she had plugged in the day before. The numbers flashed twelve. She felt like she had just fallen asleep. Had she been dreaming? It was at the tip of her mind. Ah, yes. The motorcycle. Flying through the air. Falling.

Vaguely recalling the motorcycle ride, the memory faded from her mind as quickly as it had returned, and she drifted back to sleep.

CHAPTER
SEVEN

"Every good and perfect gift is from above,
coming down from the Father of the heavenly lights,
who does not change like shifting shadows."

– James 1:17

Jimmy Pollaski

The sound of my voice disperses. The scenes close in around me, forming a tunnel of astounding radiance. The hospital—my home—my family—disappear into a carton of memory. A small wave of sadness washes over me. Leaving them behind, I know I cannot turn back. The light possesses such an irresistible calm it beckons me ahead. Am I moving? The world around me fades to light, yet I am alive— more Now than ever before.

Just as the tunnel appears to be never-ending, the light

gives way to a figure emanating rays of unnamable color. Is this Him? No, He is all around. In the energy pulsating through me. God—Spirit—the Source of All that Is. I sense His hand on my shoulder like a Father welcoming His son home after a long trip across the country. Like the warm embrace of a Mother overflowing with unconditional Love. It feels as though I never left.

Examining my hands, I recognize that I have been reduced to energy; I am weightless, radiating light like the figure advancing toward me. I am still wearing my blue jeans tattered at the knees, and my blue-and-white-striped shirt that I dressed in that morning. Tears push through my eyes. I try to wipe them away, but I feel nothing but warmth and the absence of space.

This is the transition between physicality to spirit, I hear a voice whisper. *The feeling of confinement vanishes when the mirage of time stops.*

The light being shifts, and I realize that I'm staring into the comforting features of my grandmother. She smiles, raising her hands to my face. Her laugh immediately thrusts me back to the time when I'm five years old, and she's handing me a bucket of cookies. As I generously shove them into my mouth, her eyes water with amusement. She looks like she did years ago, gray curly hair just past her shoulders, blue eyes sparkling, and her slender frame hunched over. Her skin is covered in wrinkles.

"Nonna," I say.

"James. It is so wonderful to have you back." Her soundless words come from within my mind.

"You, too," I say. I'm surprised that I have also communicated telepathically.

Without warning, another memory surfaces. I'm falling

asleep on my grandmother's brown pullout couch the night that I hid from my mother in a drunken stupor. I'm sixteen years old. As I slide into a dream state, my grandmother passes away from a sudden stroke, unrelated to her concern for my intoxicated condition. I had not caused her death, I realize. It was her time.

Now as she stands before me, she's wearing the same flowered dress that she wore nine years ago as I hugged her goodnight. Her face lights up.

"I appear the same as the day I died so that when loved ones cross over, they'll remember me from the last point where our lives crossed paths," she says.

Just as the explanation enters my mind, the elderly lady transforms into a petite young woman with glowing blonde curls cascading down her back. Her skin is as smooth as a pebble endlessly caressed by the sea. Bright yellow light emanates from her being.

"When you knew me I was your Nonna, Josephine Redmond. But here, James, we exist in our most radiant form. We are beings of energy and light, able to instantly transform into whatever look we please."

Examining my arms, I notice the cuts from my accident have disappeared. Am I breathing? No, there is no oxygen here. I attempt to hold this idea solid in my own hands. But nothing is solid either, not even these two hands. My 25-year-old hands skilled at stretching the boundary between safety and danger. The hands which spent years marinating steak, turning the pages of countless cookbooks, writing out statistics for Business class. Hands which have taken the blunt from the hands of others, lifting it to my lips and clearing the air of smoke. The very same hands grasping the handles of the motorcycle with such a tight grip, they're aching. No, there is no more pain. Pain is contrary to the boundary of the body, and these lines are fading, fusing the past with the present moment.

"Things are vibrating much faster in this realm. There is no past and future. There is only the Now," Josephine says. "You're still in shock from your quick transition, but within you, you know everything I'm telling you. It lives in your cells. In your soul memory. You must fully shed your mortal mechanisms to remember."

Josephine points to the watch on my wrist. I look down and notice the hands are frozen in place at eleven-nineteen in the morning. I watch the numbers disintegrate into the black background before the entire watch evaporates from my wrist.

"No time has passed since you were last here because time is merely an illusion. Twenty-five years is comparable to the blink of an eye."

"I feel changes in me, but I'm fighting them," I say. "So many images of my life are flashing around me. I see my mother's sad face the first day I climbed aboard the bus for kindergarten. I see her crying as I lay unconscious in the hospital. She's throwing her arms in the air, yelling at a young girl in the nursing home. And then I see my friends waiting for me to pick up beer on my way home from work last week. In another image, they're helping my parents pack things into boxes, and they're on a flight back to California from my funeral, all at the same time. If I focus, I can hear their voices clearly, like I'm right there next to them. I promised to let them know…"

"Once you review your life in its entirety, you'll realize everything you've gained and lost from your experiences. It'll be much easier to let them go. See how everything glimmers ceaselessly, untouched by death and decay?" She raises her arms upward. "Look around!"

I smile, admiring the familiar awe of my surroundings. The path's entrance channels into an immense garden which runs for miles on end with flowers of every kind—hydrangeas, lilies, roses, each as bright as the memory of a firm gaze into the sun. Flowered vines spill over sparkling fountains and weave through the railings of a bridge. The stream below flows into a glassy lake. The garden subsides into a brick courtyard. Beyond that, a wide staircase leads to an edifice supported by two white pillars. People are mingling on the marble ledges, which elevate as the staircase rises. Are they waiting for me? I notice each person is surrounded with an aura of brightly colored light.

"Come," Josephine says. And without even taking a step, we're standing on the marble floor amidst the crowd.

"How did we—"

"Shhh, listen to your inner-self. You already know."

Examining the crowd, I realize they're not just a group of strangers, but those I once believed to have lost forever: my Grandpa Paul, and my Grandma Eloise from my father's side of the family. My friends: Eleanor Mancott, Aberash Fumnanya, and others I have known—not only in my most recent life, but also from many of my lives from centuries previous. They're all rejoicing at my return.

Another woman steps out from behind Josephine, waving eagerly. It is Emily, my mother's close friend who lost a battle with breast cancer five years before my grandmother's death. Suddenly, a flashback of my mother consumes me. Her blonde hair is matted down around her face from her tears, which flow harder every time she sees the picture frame she turned over on the wooden mantel. I'm eleven in this memory and can't quite understand the gravity of the situation. Now I recognize that it is a picture of Emily, her smile face-down on the windowsill.

"It's good to have you back," she says. I smile, nodding, although I know we're both thinking about my mother.

As I continue embracing each person in a transfer of warmth unlike physical contact, I immediately stop at a woman of Native American descent called Dezba. I remember having chosen her as my spiritual guide for my brief time on Earth—a disguised, intuitive voice, whispering words of advice and warning as I spun through life's motions.

Her lips form a thin, toothless beam, a smile of comfort and patience from her last lifetime as a Navajo, nurturing eight children within her tribe's boundaries. I recall how my past life intertwined with hers when I was her youngest son called Johonaei. In that life, I remember that Patricia, then known as Haloke, was my eldest sister. She had grown very close to me helping my mother take care of her young ones. A memory of the night Halaoke was kidnapped by a Mexican army flashes before my eyes. I feel her heartache as she is torn from our family, forced to work as a slave, but this story is one of the past and so I quickly push it from my mind.

Dezba's hair, like long dark straw, surrounds the soft features of her face—her almond eyes, skin saturated in freckles brightened by years spent in the sun. She looks exactly as I last saw her before I had entered my new body, secure within my mother's womb. I recall the stories Dezba murmured to me then, about a boy with a voice so powerful the whole world would one day hear his words from beyond. Patricia clutches her hand to her belly as my foot kicks from the other side. She's singing songs to hush her hidden child.

"James," Dezba says, her voice pushing away the recollections.

"Dezba."

"I'm so sorry I couldn't warn you of impending danger,"

Dezba says. "Now and then, when death happens suddenly, human emotions like shock, grief, and resentment engulf us, making the transition into this dimension complex. It's important for you to understand your life was cut short because your most recent chapter came to a close. It was one of the many probable paths you had aligned for your life, but it was an experience pertinent to your soul's expansion."

"I know," I say. "My accident couldn't have been prevented. It was my time."

Her expression softens. "Let me take you to the Council who will walk you through your life review. You'll better understand everything then."

Dezba takes my hand, guiding me away from the brilliant backdrop which stretches out in the vast expanse behind me. She leads me across a stone path surrounded by vines of the deepest green. Our steps continue from the marble floor to soft, pure soil. I look around, struck by the beautiful, flawless landscape. I'm still in a state of shock, though it is filled with peacefulness. The air tastes of jasmine, and I feel the sweet tune of birds singing in the distance. My senses muddled, I realize they're no longer connected to a physical body.

I look up, noticing the sun absent from the sky. Regardless, the firmament appears in an assortment of energetic colors—violet, rose, yellow and peach, which linger in a soft shade of light. The air is temperate and easy, taking on the eternal warmth of a tropical island. We are no longer aboard a planet, abiding by the laws of Earth. Day will not fade to night, nor summer to fall. Instead, particles of light resembling stars perpetually twinkle through an atmosphere of unfathomable glory. To my right, I catch a glimpse of white-capped mountains rising above a massive field of tall, green grass, swaying in a soft breeze.

As we walk slowly down the path, Dezba waves her hand through the air. A pair of butterflies materializes from her grasp like a magic trick I remember having seen as a child. In this recollection, I'm barely two years old, clinging tightly to my mother's leg as the magician at our church fair swoops his hat above my head. Out soar the butterflies, their orange and black wings dancing. "Monarchs," my mother says. I let go of her leg, reaching up to catch one. Instead of perching it on my finger, I enclose the whole butterfly in my hand, crushing its wings as it falls to floor. I crouch down, eager to make it fly again. My mother grabs my wrist. "You hurt it. It's not alive anymore," she says in a heated tone. My chubby face looks up into hers, curious, because her words are familiar, even though she tells me I won't understand what death is.

"Is this them?" I ask.

"Yes," Dezba says. "These are the butterflies you witnessed years ago. As you can see, they are alive and well."

The butterflies flutter away, landing on a picture frame above Dezba's head. The painting is the same one hung over my mother's bed, called *Monet's Garden Path at Giverny.* I realize we are no longer outdoors, but inside the enormous white building where my friends gather. The breadth of the room spans further than my eyes can follow. The walls are adorned with endless paintings, bookcases, fireplaces, and vines spotted with blossoming flowers hanging from the mantles. More doors dot the length of the wall between the decorations, leading to further libraries.

I know that we're in the Hall of Records, where the Council of Elders waits for me. Dezba ushers me up a spiral staircase so steep it appears we will never reach the top. After climbing only a few steps, we enter a vast hallway lit by thick candles, burning in sheer animation.

"Here." Dezba points to a brown door with leaves carved around the edges. Without opening it, I'm inside the room, surrounded by a dome of bright light. In front of me, several men and women with sparkling white hair are sitting at a long rectangular table. They are dressed in velvet maroon robes, golden pendants hanging from their necks. Their facial features are soft, humble. I know they are not here to judge me, but to help me recognize how the events in my life both strengthened and broke down my soul.

Suddenly, the walls become a colossal theater.

The Elder sitting at the center of the table speaks. "Every event in your life pushes you in the direction of unearthing your true, Divine Self. By analyzing your actions from afar, you will understand how your choices led you to the places you needed to go to remember what you set out to experience during this lifetime."

Although my soul does not completely take residence in my body until the later stages of my mother's pregnancy, I watch my most recent life officially begin the moment I open my eyes to the world—the nurse wrapping me in the soft, green blanket Emily has given my mother as a gift. My father looks down at me, beaming, as I stretch out my tiny, new fingers. All at once, I feel every sensation of each person around me. My mother's exhaustion; my father's contentment as he holds his healthy first-born son; my sister's anxiousness. She bounces on the couch beside my grandmother, awaiting the news that the baby girl expected is actually a brother. The cold air against my face.

Every single moment of my entire life plays out across the vast, globular screen; surround sound booms in my ears. Every little bit of pain and joy echoes within my being—my thick head of dark hair turns blond as my infant body grows bigger, prone position to my feet. I'm stumbling to a stand on wobbly legs, learning the hurt of falling face-first as I climb over the barrier of my crib. I feel my lip protruding, like the time when I am six years old. My ten-year-old sister flies across the room as I yank a toy truck from her hands. I watch how my choice to inflict pain on someone else results in pain for both parties. Regardless of my sister's mild temperament, she shoves me into a rocking chair. My tooth knocks into my upper lip as the blood pours out onto my shirt, staining the off-white carpet deep crimson. I understand in retrospect the weight of cause and effect, how even the most miniscule action shifts the energy of the people around me. Each choice I've made illuminates the power of my free will, its ability to dramatize or water-down the inevitable—cementing future possibilities into the present moment. My choices fill in the outline of my life story, which I remember having written in a large white room in this very building, before my birth turned the first page to the next chapter.

A week before my ninth birthday, my mother hides a new bicycle in the closet. I find it the next day when my mother goes out to lunch. With my father busy at work in the back yard, I choose to take it for a spin without them knowing. I can feel my mother's worry as she searches the house and I'm nowhere to be found; I see the car that would've crossed my path had I not been pulled down by a powerful force I am not aware of. The bicycle hits a rock and flies out from under me. Pain shoots up my arm as it lands in an unnatural angle under the bicycle's spokes. This incident is just one of my life's painful events. I continue to watch the discomfort I inflict on myself, many more times.

I watch Coach William throw his fists in the air, determined to win the National Middle School Cross Country

Championship. The hope of every athlete around me pushing fifteen miles pulsates throughout my body. I'm overwhelmed by the agony of an opponent who topples to the ground on the final mile, clutching his knee after I nonchalantly trip him to take first place. The yellow tapeline falls, my lungs dying for air. It's the guilt of winning something I know I don't deserve that kills me more after the entire city praises my success.

I watch how the incident leads me to volunteer for the Run for Cancer two years later. I'm fifteen years old when I run the twenty-mile route, ending with a swim in the Atlantic Ocean on that cold November day. I swear the stinging in my lungs will be my end as I struggle to swim, panic scrolling through my mind. How could I volunteer myself for death? A stranger yanks me by the waist through the ice-cold ocean as my body goes into shock. Minutes later, I'm wrapped in a towel, shivering uncontrollably—alive.

Only as I review the circumstances do I witness the transformation of the cancer patients affected by our run, the impact of our choice to donate not so much our money, but our energy. How the mere acts of positive thought and prayer transform into positive results.

I continue to observe times in my life where my love has healed, how my hatred has broken people down. I see myself at sixteen, sitting on the lifeguard stand beside Ashley Korlan. I'm leaning in for an awkward first kiss as her face glows in the light of the moon. I see the fight between Joey Svensson over whose crush started first. Fists to jaw, skin wet with salty tears, and laughter a year later at the foolishness of our immaturity.

My final years of high school play around me. The endless hours of homework followed by sleepless nights, and our weekend celebrations at the quarry, ravaging our bodies with mass amounts of alcohol. Running home in wet clothes, yelling in the empty streets. I see my hand rubbing Eddie's back as he desperately holds the toilet bowl. Eddie is smiling months later as he reveals his brilliant plan to move away together, the California heat beckoning us to escape the New England snowstorms and the reckless days of our youth, the familiarity of a city we've outgrown. Not by coincidence, his friend has extra rooms in an apartment, fifteen minutes outside of downtown San Diego. The apartment just so happens to be fifteen minutes from the University of San Diego, where I've been accepted to the School of Business Department. My childhood dreams of opening my own restaurant can now come true.

I see my mother crying as I wave goodbye from the terminal in Logan Airport. Eddie is in front of me, already halfway down the jet bridge. A smirk stretches across his face. I call to my mother as the attendant scans my ticket. My words resound through the speakers: "I'll be okay, Mom." Her sadness eats away at me as the scenes replay. Why is she so distraught? She knows I'll be back home to visit for Christmas, six months from this point.

My life review pauses.

"One major theme in your mother's life is to rise above the false notion of loss," the Chief Guide's voice rumbles. "She must let go in order to develop. She seeks to remember that loss is not real, regardless if we appear to be losing people and things every day. This includes pieces of ourselves. As we shed our skin, new skin cells are produced. Nothing is ever lost. Instead, we replenish."

"Am I reminding her of that?"

"You are. You will remind many, even from here. We do this by infusing knowledge in the minds of those on Earth, which filters through their thoughts. They must learn to differentiate guidance from the overpowering Ego."

"I promised I would let them know I'm okay, but how can I, if they don't know it's me?"

"You cannot give them too much knowledge directly, because they must learn from the experiences in their own lives. Guidance is around them, if they choose to accept it. In order to maintain the mystery of life, we will very softly murmur the secret of immortality—and try our best to make sure those on Earth finish out their plan without creating the end prematurely."

"What happens if they do?"

"In some cases, it's their time. Other instances, it's an egotistical act that may affect what the soul chooses to experience in lives to come. Many recognize this in hindsight."

"It couldn't happen to my mother, could it? I still feel so close to her, but she doesn't respond. I'm here at the same time. She's oblivious, but there is a girl around her at the nursing home who looks straight at me. Can she hear me?"

"She does hear you. You know that. If she chooses, she can hear me now too. Her knowledge is limited. I will give you the outline of her life so you will know how your stories can connect. Together you will help people overcome loss, even if the feat seems implausible."

"Okay. So what is my life theme?"

"It is exactly what you are seeing. A brief yet fulfilling life of perseverance."

"Almost like every day of my life I died a new death."

"Every day of your life you lived to prove death's delusion."

"Yes. I never died, did I?"

"You know, your heart still beats."

The pause button is released. I feel my heart thudding in

my chest as the plane takes off for California. I'm going to watch until the final moment, and rewind again. I'll replay it many times, and talk about what I might have done better in this life, though in essence I know everything has happened as it should.

"Yes, my heart still beats."

CHAPTER
EIGHT

Patricia Pollaski

Thursday -- February 26th -- 5:42 a.m.

T he last thing Patricia remembered before falling asleep was the clock rolling past four a.m. Now the phone was blaring in her ear, even though her alarm was set for after seven. The sun had yet to peek through the curtains.

She had been dreaming again. Her heart hammered in her chest as she leaned over to pick up the phone, the covers slipping off her shoulders.

"Hello?" she mumbled, her voice cracking.

"Mom, it's me."

"Jimmy?"

"No, Mom. It's Denise."

Patricia wiped her eyes, aching from lack of sleep. "Denise. I'm sorry, I'm half awake."

"No, it's my fault for calling so early. Eric had to go out of town last minute and I'm frantic. I need someone to take Anna while I'm teaching. I know the residents would love her, so I thought maybe she could go with you to the nursing home. Just during the days this week, and I'll come get her in the evenings."

Patricia sighed. "I'd love to, but you know how hard it is for me to keep track of the residents I have now. Simply getting myself out of the house is a chore."

"But Mrs. Marietta loved it when you took us to work. They all did. And you know Anna is the most well behaved four-year-old there is."

Before Patricia knew what she was saying, she agreed.

"Thank you. I'll have her there in an hour."

Patricia's head sunk into her pillow. Anxiety resurfaced in her chest. Still lying flat, she reached her arm back to grab her alarm clock, which she usually kept beside the phone, but she could only find the receiver.

"Argh," she grumbled as she sat up. The radio clock had been moved completely behind the phone base on the other side of the table. She leaned around to read the bold, red numbers: Five fifty-two. *Still more time to sleep*, she thought. Yet she knew she risked having another nightmare.

The terrifying dreams woke her up with the feeling that the images in her mind had been real. In her last few hours of sleep she dreamt of Jimmy holding tight to her arms as he dangled over the side of a cliff, the surf a menacing whirlpool below. His voice was muted. No matter how hard she tried, her arms were too weak to yank him up. As his grasp loosened, she felt him slip away. Down he went, his body flailing into a sea-spray abyss.

My fault. If only I could have pulled him up.

85

Patricia reminded herself that it was only a dream. No matter how genuine his hands felt, they were not his hands. She did not let him go. *Cannot let go*, she thought.

Patricia continued to drift in and out of sleep until a loud pounding on the front door roused her. She pulled herself to her feet. Throwing her robe on over her nightgown, she leaned under the bed to recover a slipper, the other not visible.

"Screw it," she muttered. She stumbled around the clothes collecting on the bedroom floor and headed down the stairs, wearing only one slipper. The floor was cold against the bottom of her bare foot.

The knocking persisted. Patricia squinted, allowing her eyes to adjust to the light as she made her way through the living room. Her husband had left the track lights on full blast. Outside, the sky was clouded over.

"Come in, Denise," she called, but realized as she reached the door that it was locked. She struggled to turn the lock, spinning it in every direction before it gave way.

"I'm sorry. Dad doesn't usually lock the door. You know how it sticks sometimes." Patricia leaned over to hug her daughter who moved forward stiffly, her blue dress-suit limiting the mobility of her slender frame.

"I remember the time that Jimmy and I locked Dad out and we couldn't let him back in."

Patricia didn't say anything. Her mind drifted as she watched a crow land on a tree branch above them. She recalled the jog down the stairs from her office room, years ago. She too had struggled with the lock as her children laughed behind her, her husband drenched in the rain.

"Grammy P!" the tiny girl's voice cried, sliding Patricia out of her trance. Anna tilted her head back in order to meet Patricia's eyes. Blonde curls poked out from under her pink hat.

"My little treasure," Patricia said. "How I missed you so." Anna locked her small arms around Patricia's leg.

"Anna, hun, let go. Grammy's getting old," Denise said. "You don't want to detach her leg. She is supposed to take care of you today, not the other way around."

"Sorry," Anna said, shimmying backward. Her face contorted into a sulk before brightening up a second later. "Grammy, meet my Dolly. That's her name. I gave it to her."

"I love it, honey" Patricia said. Her attention diverted as the crow took off, cawing into the gray sky.

"You go inside with Grammy now and show her all of your new toys," Denise urged, gently pushing her daughter forward. "I have to go now, I'm already late!"

"Goodbye, Denise," Patricia said, bending down as far as her knees would allow. "Say bye to Mommy." Together they waved as Anna jumped up and down through Patricia's arms.

"Now what, now what? Dolly wants to play!"

Patricia sighed, picking Anna up into her right arm. She struggled to hold the door open with her other hand as the girl squirmed.

Patricia still needed to tell Mrs. Marietta that she would have a follower the next couple of days. She had to change her clothes and make breakfast, all while entertaining the four-year-old. Already, she felt her energy level sinking.

"Sit on the couch for now, Anna, and Grammy'll play soon. She has some important things to take care of, okay?"

Anna had already begun pulling her dolls, teacups, stuffed animals, and other random accessories out of her blue knapsack, talking to herself in different voices.

Patricia picked up the phone to call her boss. She expected an irritated response, having such a young girl tag along. She knew the dangers of small hands around intricate medical equipment and frail senior citizens. Mrs. Marietta's indifference startled her. Someone had messed with the scheduling and there were additional staff members clocked in that morning. Patricia wouldn't have to come in until the afternoon.

Things have a way of working out, Patricia thought, her nerves settling. She had until two o'clock to wear out Anna enough so she would nap during her work shift.

Instead of getting the girl's attention, Patricia sat down on the couch, watching Anna feed her dolls invisible food. Patricia's eyelids fluttered. Her motivation to move diminished. She thought of the long day ahead of her. Changing diapers, feeding people without teeth, folding laundry. She cursed out loud.

-- 1:59 p.m. --

Patricia seized Anna's hand as they entered the empty nursing home lobby, the girl's bag dragging along the floor.

"Smells like fishies," Anna said with a giggle.

Patricia breathed in the strong smell of rubbing alcohol. A rush of nostalgia swept over her. "Well, look at the fishies over there in that tank. Why don't you go check them out?"

"Okay, let's go, Nemo!" Anna cried, yanking out her orange stuffed fish. She left the rest of her toys in a heap on the ground. Patricia pulled off her granddaughter's hat and coat as the girl fidgeted.

"Calm yourself," Patricia said. She tucked the accessories

into the jacket sleeve as Anna darted for the tank, her curls bouncing at her cheeks.

Patricia headed toward the office to deposit the winter gear into the closet, keeping one eye on her granddaughter. Just as she approached the doorway, the lobby door beside it swung open. A girl hurried by, knocking into Patricia's arm. Patricia recognized her, but could not place how she knew her.

"Oh, excuse me. I'm sorry," the girl said, rushing toward the exit. She glanced over her shoulder in an abrupt motion.

Patricia stared. As the door closed, a cold draft blew across the room.

Anna danced to the bell ringing. "More, Grammy, more!" She twirled around the room, holding her fish by its fins.

"Settle down now. We're going to take care of other grammys and grampas who don't have the ability to dance like you. Please, my dear." Patricia pointed to a row of chairs beside the fish tank.

Pouting, Anna did as she was told.

Mrs. Marietta pushed through the lobby door. Out of breath, she too nearly knocked into Patricia. "Oh, good. You're here. Some folks are in the game room, but Mrs. Gedolewen stayed behind and needs an attendant." As she spoke, Mrs. Marietta watched Anna stand on the chair, her forehead pressed against the glass, intently following the creatures swimming by. "Cute," Mrs. Marietta said. "Now get to work."

"Right," Patricia said.

Patricia guided Anna down the hall. They found Mrs. Gedolewen in her wheelchair, back turned toward the door. Her white hair was matted down, her hands folded in her lap. Outside, the sun's rays spilled out from behind dispersing clouds.

Anna pulled her arm from Patricia's grasp, plopping to

the ground.

"Is everything okay, Mrs. Gedolewen?" Patricia asked, reaching Mrs. Gedolewen's side.

"Yes. The day's brightening," she answered, her words barely reaching a whisper.

"Ah, good ol' New England weather for you. Did you know it's supposed to reach sixty degrees tomorrow? In February!" Patricia said. "Is it okay if I turn you around? I have someone here I'd like you to meet." Patricia spun the chair around even though the old woman didn't answer. "An extra visitor today. This is my granddaughter, Anna."

Anna hid her face between her hands.

"My granddaughter," Mrs. Gedolewen echoed. She stared beyond the girl resting on the floor, her eyes glossy.

"Yes. Anna," Patricia repeated.

Still staring off into space, thick creases formed at the corners of Mrs. Gedolewen's eyes as she released a thin smile. "We sat in my room all day today."

"I'm sorry, you could've rang the office for someone to pick you up."

"Well, the truth is, it was the best day of my life." Mrs. Gedolewen laughed. "And to think, I didn't even have much for lunch."

"I can ring the kitchen for you and have them fix something up. What would you like?" Patricia hurried over to the phone on the table between the beds. As she reached for the receiver, her hand slid across the top of a glass jar filled with change set in front of the phone. The metal lid felt cold against her skin.

"Thank you. A tuna sandwich would be nice. Oh, and don't forget to order some cookies for Anna's tea party."

Anna's head perked up. "I gots my tea set right here,

Misses," she said. She dumped out the contents of her bag, the plastic teacups bouncing across the floor. Anna slid on her knees to recover one before it rolled beneath the bed.

"Anna, be care—" Patricia cut herself off. Her sharp tone eased as she spoke into the phone. "Yes, can I have a tuna sandwich and some cookies sent to room 17, please? Thanks a bunch." Slamming down the receiver, she bent down to gather the toys scattered around the floor. She pointed to the corner of the room. "Over there, Anna. You and your toys. You need to stay out of the way so nobody trips over you. Please be good for Grammy."

The girl erupted in a fit of sniffles. Her lip curled under as she scooted her bottom across the floor.

"It's okay, child. Don't be so gloomy. You have a tea party to host, and tears will only make your tea salty."

"Yes, Misses. Lemon Strawberry Apple tea for Nemo and Dolly and Grammy, and for you, too."

"Miriam, child. Call me Miriam."

"Okay, Misses Miriam." Anna grinned. She arranged her toys in a line, counting the white flowered teacups she placed in front of them.

Patricia watched Anna from the corner of her eye as she wheeled the chair around to maneuver Mrs. Gedolewen onto the bed. As she did so, exhaustion overwhelmed Patricia's body, but she kept her chin raised to prove to herself otherwise. If she didn't constantly think about her fatigue, she wouldn't be so tired. It was as simple as that. Patricia adjusted the pillows as Mrs. Gedolewen settled atop the blanket.

"Somebody should've made hips better than this. So you don't ever have to replace them! Sure is a pain in the butt," Mrs. Gedolewen said. "Just to let you know, it's when a person's tired that they're more likely to hurt themselves. And you, my dear, are certainly in need of more rest. I can see it in your face." She held up a bony finger.

"I'll be fine. Don't worry about me."

Mrs. Gedolewen's glasses sank further down her nose, revealing her blue eyes. "I do. But everything will get better in time. What you really need is a good bedtime story, to help you doze off. You can't really concentrate on the story, though. You just have to let it pass by your ears like the wind catching the trees."

"I wish I had someone to tell me stories. I don't know if my husband would be up for it. He's snoring before I put my head down."

The older woman's face brightened. "Ah, but we're all filled with stories living within our bones. If we listen to the distant, inner voices beyond our thoughts, we can drift off to the constant, never-ending story replaying in our heads. If you're quiet enough, you can hear it. The story of who you are, and why." She paused, taking a deep breath, then continued. "The fall I took in my icy driveway nearly killed me. My hip smashed into a million pieces, and I had no family around to help. Although I had to deal with massive amounts of pain on my own, I know that tragedy, when it happens, moves us along in life. It leads us places and strengthens us. There are no accidents, Patricia. If the fall hadn't happened, my daughter wouldn't be here now."

"You have a daughter? I thought she—"

"You're right. A daughter I haven't seen in twenty-five years. What kind of daughter is that? Runs away to get married at nineteen. Doesn't tell me about my own granddaughter. Doesn't even help me move into the nursing home. She's selfish, insecure, and most of all stubborn. But she's human, and she's my child, and I know she'll be here in time. There's a certain timing to everything, you know. Can't force anything in life. They always come back to us in the end."

Patricia's demeanor saddened. "Not all of them."

"You'd be surprised."

"So where is she?" Patricia asked.

"Erin? Oh, I know it'll take her another couple of days to get here. And probably not by her own will."

Anna's chatting danced across the room. "Yes, yes, your cookies will be here soon, little Dolly!" Shifting into a high-pitched voice, she continued, "Thank you, Princess Anna. Ohhh, Jimmy. So glad you can join us!"

Patricia turned her head around. She watched Anna stir coins around in her cup.

"I thought you were all the ways in California. But my mama says you went really far away." The girl's small hands danced in all directions before pretending to sip her tea.

A sharp sting pierced through Patricia's body. "Anna, who in the world are you talking to? And where did you get those pennies? Be careful you don't swallow them, for goodness' sake."

"Uncle Jimmy came all the ways from California for my tea party!"

"But Jimmy is gone, he's dead," Patricia snapped without thinking what she was saying. She ran her fingers under her eyelids. Even then, she couldn't prevent her tears from moistening her cheeks. "How do I explain death to a four-year-old?" she asked, half to herself.

"You'd be surprised that sometimes kids know more about death than adults do. Most of us lose it sometime during our very early childhood." Mrs. Gedolewen's gaze transfixed to the corner of the room, her eyes regaining their dream-like quality.

"Lose what?"

The old woman didn't answer.

"Lose what?" Patricia repeated.

"As the childhood imagination fades, the need for the concrete sets in. Most kids lose their supernatural abilities as their everyday contact with the world consumes them. The conditioning of society takes over."

"Huh? I have no idea what you're talking about," Patricia said, irritated. "And where in the world is the food? We've been waiting for an hour now. You'd think a tuna sandwich would only be a few minutes." She hurried over to the phone. Just as she picked it up, the door swung open. Mrs. Marietta held a plate of food and a basket of cookies.

"Cookies!" Anna cried, clapping her hands.

Tossing down the receiver, this time Patricia's hand hit the jar, flinging it off the table with a crash. Pennies and shards of glass flew in every direction.

"Shit," Patricia swore, immediately covering her mouth. "I am so sorry. I don't know what's wrong with me. I just—I can't do anything right." She brushed the remnants together with her shoe, weeping. "Anna, please don't move. There's glass everywhere."

Mrs. Marietta rested the food on the empty bed. "It's okay, Patricia. Calm down." She went into the closet to fetch a broom and a dustpan. Grabbing the trashcan, she began sweeping up the mess of glass.

"I don't feel like myself anymore. This just isn't me." Patricia's face was warm with tears. "Don't worry, I will find all of your pennies. Get a new jar."

"Don't worry about that. Plenty more where that came from!" Mrs. Gedolewen said. "It's just change my husband sent me over the years to enrich my life. Nothing big or anything, but you know, sometimes it's the small things in life that count most."

"That is nice," Patricia said, although she missed what the woman had said after her first few words.

Thoughts engulfed her mind. Heavy sobs shook her body. On top of finding every coin and speck of glass, she still had to make sure the little girl didn't get into any more trouble. She had to make sure the tuna sandwich made it into the old woman's mouth, even though Patricia could barely open her own mouth to speak coherently.

"Patricia, let me clean this up," Mrs. Marietta said in a firm tone. "Take the rest of the day off. Seriously, there's no need to get flustered."

"What?"

"Go home and rest. Come in tomorrow."

"Sure." She closed her eyes, cupping her hands together over her nose. The darkness brought with it a memory of Jimmy smudging chocolate cookie over his face at the County Fair. Her eyes popped open. "Anna, get your things together now, please. We're going home."

Silently, the girl put her toys into her bag. Patricia bent over to grab her hand. As they walked to the door, a piece of glass crunched beneath her sneaker.

"It's okay, Grammy P. Please don't cry," Anna said in a loud whisper. "He just wanted to share some tea."

Mrs. Marietta handed Patricia the basket of cookies. Mrs. Gedolewen waved feebly.

"I'll get some sleep," Patricia said, squeezing Anna's hand, and the two headed out the door.

--5:48 p.m.--

Patricia sat on the couch, one arm around her granddaughter. "This little piggy went to the park. This little piggy went to school. And this little piggy, he went to the market," she said, pulling on the girl's toes.

"To get some cookies!" Anna exclaimed.

"Well, okay, but he has to eat his dinner first."

Patricia glanced at her watch, her stomach grumbling. The chicken had only been in the oven for five minutes.

"And this little piggy went to his bed to take a nap," Anna said, hugging her elbows. Smashing her face into Patricia's shoulder, she made snoring sounds.

"Ah, yes. This little piggy was wide awake all day long hosting her tea party. Now she is mighty tired."

Anna didn't respond. Her small face relaxing, Patricia knew her granddaughter would be asleep in no time. Resting her eyes, Patricia leaned her head back against the couch. *Only for a minute.*

The day's events played out. She saw the jar falling to the ground in slow motion. She saw Mrs. Gedolewen's pale face, the creases marking her wisdom. She heard the woman's gentle voice. Only in her mind's eye did she see Jimmy, sipping a cup of tea, a smile bending his lips. Everything uniting, and then fading.

--7:09 p.m.--

Patricia awoke to the sound of heavy footsteps. Weary, she sat up straight, wiping the drool from her chin. Where was she? She remembered her granddaughter sitting on her lap. Her arms were empty now. Pulling herself to her feet, she looked around the living room but Anna was nowhere in sight.

"Patricia, wake up!" her husband yelled from around the corner.

"Shit, shit, shit," she said, hurrying into the hallway. "Where is she?" The sound of running water crashed against the bathtub's smooth surface.

Patricia found them in the bathroom. Her husband lifted Anna out of the bathtub, which was half filled with water. Her jeans, soaked up to the knees, dripped into a puddle on the floor. The drain moaned.

"I just wanted to see if Nemo could swim like the other fishies," Anna cried.

Jim shot Patricia an angry look.

"We fell asleep," Patricia stated firmly. "We were sitting right over there on the couch. And that's the last thing I remember. Anna and I were both sleeping." She squatted down to remove Anna's wet jeans. "Honey, being in the bathtub by yourself is dangerous, you know that."

"I'm sorry." Anna's head sunk down as she sobbed.

Briefly looking up at her husband, Patricia saw dark blue veins emerging at his temples. "Patricia, you need to be more careful. You should have been watching her."

"Oh, don't go and start that again. I slept two hours last night. You sit here and act like you're all fine and dandy. Like you didn't just lose your son. Don't you feel anything?"

"Of course I do. You don't think I'm hurting just as much as you? But Jimmy isn't alive anymore, Patricia, and Anna is. There is nothing we can do but pick ourselves up and keep going."

"Right. I have to go take the chicken out of the oven, because I think it's burning." Patricia turned, allowing the tears to rush down her cheeks without reservation.

On her way to the kitchen, a sharp knock startled her. Her daughter pushed open the door just as Patricia passed by.

"Mom, are you okay? Why are you crying?"

Patricia sucked in a gulp of air before speaking. "I'm fine. Anna got a little wet, but she's fine. Except that she needs a new pair of pants. Oh, and dinner is ready."

"You need any help?"

"No," Patricia said. "Go take care of your daughter. Get ready for dinner."

Patricia lowered the oven door, the heat pouring into her face. Grabbing two dishtowels from the oven handle, she wiped the rest of her tears before lifting the chicken onto the burners.

The bird had darkened around the edges. As she pulled the towels out from under the dish, one side stuck, the hot glass sliding against her thumb. Patricia cursed, raising her hand to her lips. The saliva eased the burn only a bit, the sting piercing through her skin. Patricia's stomach groaned. Throwing the towels onto the counter, she collapsed into her chair at the dinner table, cooling her thumb against her tongue.

As her eyes shut, she began dozing off. The other chairs shifted, scratching the floor. She lifted her head up.

Her husband and daughter took their regular seats—Jim at the head of the table next to Patricia's right arm. Denise was to the right of him, stacking up phone books for Anna to sit on in the seat adjacent to her.

Patricia forced herself not to look over at Jimmy's seat, tucked tightly against the table.

CHAPTER
NINE

Lorrena Shaw

Thursday -- February 26th -- 7:10 a.m.

Her mother gripped the steering wheel, staring intently at the road. Lorrena glared at her mother, but she did not turn her head.

"The nursing home is up here on the right," Lorrena said.

"You're going to school, Lorrena."

"I know, I'm just saying."

Lorrena listened to the car's engine humming as she counted the streetlights between the nursing home and her school. To her surprise, there were only ten.

Her mother turned left into the parking lot of Gloucester High School, stopping the car in front of the white cement steps leading to the school's entrance. Reaching into her purse, she pulled out a paper folded neatly into a square. Smoothing it out, she handed it to Lorrena.

"Here's your schedule. There's a bus that will take you home around two p.m. Have a good day." Erin leaned over to kiss Lorrena on the cheek.

"Okay, enough. See you later," Lorrena said. She opened the car door and jumped out. Her mother sped off, leaving Lorrena to decipher where to go on her own. The first block read "Homeroom" in 209, lasting fifteen minutes until she moved to English class with Mr. Kearney.

Making her way down the vacant corridors, the voices bounced inside her head. There were only a few students dispersed throughout the long hallway shoving things into their lockers.

"Go away. Not right now," Lorrena said softly. She pressed her fingertips to her ears, her schedule sticking out of her right hand. A boy with long brown hair raised an eyebrow at her as he slammed his locker shut.

Lorrena gave him a half-smile, still holding up her hands. Rolling his eyes, he took off in the opposite direction.

Gradually, the volume of voices diminished. "Thank God," Lorrena muttered. She hurried up the small set of stairs leading into another hallway. In front of her, she read in bold black letters: Room 209.

As Lorrena ducked around the door held open by a metal doorstop, she found a handful of students talking quietly at their desks, while others sat on top of the desk's wooden body. The teacher was nowhere in sight. Taking a seat in the back corner, Lorrena felt the other students' eyes on her. While the conversations continued shooting across the room, the voices in her mind intensified.

Lorrena closed her eyes, pretending she was the only one in the room. *No one is looking at you*, she thought to herself.

Her eyes opened to reveal the teacher in a blue dress suit

standing at the front of the classroom. Lorrena gaped in awe at the bright light that manifested above the woman's head, which slowly emerged into the young man she had seen at the nursing home. This time Lorrena could make out the striped t-shirt he wore, along with his dark blue jeans torn at the knees. His mouth moved as if he was speaking, but Lorrena couldn't decipher his words from the clutter in her mind.

"Settle down, guys. I'm sorry I'm late. Everyone please sit so I can take roll," the teacher said. "We've only got a minute before the bell rings, so let's get organized here, okay?"

Lorrena's face grew hot. The other students returned to their assigned desks, one girl giving her a weird look as she walked by. The shrill sound of the desks scraping against the floor enhanced the voices. Lorrena closed her eyes again. *Speak clearly or please shut the hell up*, she said, unsure if she had uttered the words out loud.

A distinct voice answered her request as the background noise grew silent. *Go to the home*, the voice bellowed. Although the guy's lips didn't move, she sensed the words coming from him. Keeping her focus on the figure, she felt the stares of the other students burning into her skin. *Go to the nursing home? But what if someone sees me?* she asked silently.

"Lisa, Jennifer Allen, Adam Corship." The teacher looked down at her black notebook, then back up again. "Sarah Poe, Jimmy Rowl, Chris," she called, listing the students names as they raised their hands, while others shouted, "Here!"

Lorrena shifted uneasily in her chair. The intensity of his shape faded, but the response hit her full force, as if he were talking right into her ear. *Wait for you, now*.

"Jenny Samone, Lorr—"

The bell sounded suddenly. The teacher threw her arms

up, the guy's image evaporating into the air. "Wait, everyone, almost done here. Don't leave yet!"

A mob of students had already jumped from their desks, pushing their way out the door. Lorrena ducked into the heart of the mass. The hallway was packed with kids, all carrying backpacks overflowing with books. *Right. I need to get out of here*, Lorrena thought. The crowd pushed forward, knocking her against the person in front of her. At the bottom of the steps, students dispersed into the long corridor stretching to the other end of the school where she had first entered. Instead of following them, Lorrena hustled down another level of steps. At the end of the hallway, an exit sign flickered. Without further contemplation, Lorrena rushed outside, surprised that no emergency bell sounded. Running her hand along the rough brick building, she followed the wall until she reached the front of the school where the entrance met the road. Her heart thumped in her chest.

At the corner of the sidewalk, a few kids stood in a group. One guy looked in her direction, snickering. A cigarette stuck out from between his lips. He held a lighter up to it before hiding the lighter under the bush with his pack of cigarettes. Lorrena turned her head away, darting toward the trees bordering the rim of the parking lot. Her feet ached walking as fast as her legs would carry her. Through the trees, she could make out the street and the rows of streetlights hovering over the snow-covered sidewalks.

"Let's go, kids, this isn't recess time. Get to class!" a teacher's voice called. Lorrena had already passed through the trees, the narrow path dumping her onto the road.

"Safe," she said. Although overwhelmed with relief, she glanced around to see if anyone was watching. The sidewalks, aside from the snow banks, were empty. A few cars passed by, picking up speed just after the arc in the road straightened out.

Lorrena reached into her pocket for her cell phone. After a few rings, Ariel's voice blared into her ear. "Can't answer my phone, guys, but leave me a fun message and I'll call you back!"

Lorrena frowned despite knowing her friend's schedule. They would have been together in physics class, passing notes about how Mr. Lowe's nostrils flared when he talked, revealing his enormously long nose hairs. She laughed at the thought. "Ariel, it's Lorrena. Sorry I'm laughing. Mr. Lowe is probably snorting in your face right now. You're too far away, and everyone already hates me here, I know it. Please call me soon. We really need to talk."

Lorrena shoved the phone back into her pocket. Up ahead, the bushes surrounding the walkway to the nursing home came into view. Her strides lengthened, her feet throbbing. This was it. After weeks of anticipation, she would finally come face to face with her grandmother. She had no idea what to expect, if the old woman would have any clue who she was. Luckily, Lorrena had found her grandmother's name from papers around the new house.

As Lorrena entered through the double doors of Kendall Retirement, the bell above her sounded. She froze, waiting for someone to assist her. When no one came, she peeked into a nearby room. The dining area, packed with elderly men and women, smelled of bacon. She put one hand on her stomach, empty like their kitchen cabinets. She felt in her pocket for the cash her mother had given her for the cafeteria.

Tugging on her lip with her teeth, Lorrena crept down a long corridor marked with consecutive blue doors and pictures of the ocean. She scanned the names printed below the small door knockers. The chance of finding her grandmother seemed hopeless. Uncertainty besieged her. *Could she really be waiting for me right now?* The thought slid to the back of Lorrena's mind.

A few steps later, she came upon a door held open by a wooden wedge. Lorrena stopped in her tracks, a strong sensation consuming her entire body. She could not see the name on the door, or if someone was in the room, until she stepped forward. Yet a part of her knew. The sign confirmed: Miriam Gedolewen, room 17.

The small woman rested atop her blankets, a food stand perched over her shins. Her hair, done up in tight curls, was ashen gray like the snow banks stained with mud. Her small blue eyes glistened like Lorrena's, even from far away. Lorrena stepped forward gradually, unsure of what to do next. She smiled, nervously fidgeting and shuffling her feet.

"Hello, child!" the woman said, waving her hand. "Don't be shy! You've finally made it. Close the door and come here, I've been waiting for you. Your eggs are getting cold."

"Um, hello. How did you know I was coming?" Lorrena asked timidly.

"Oh, don't be silly. Your extrasensory perception is just as keen as mine, if not fifty times better. I mean, since yours is just developing. I can see it in your eyes," she said with a smile. "But I'm sure that's nothing foreign to you."

Lorrena's mouth hung open as she stood there, dumbfounded.

"It's okay, darling, you are not crazy. Don't let anyone convince you that the visions you see aren't genuine. Come now, give your Gram a great big bear hug! Oh, and don't you worry about breaking me or anything. I just broke my hip and I won't possibly shatter anything else in the near future. It just won't happen, so I'm not afraid."

"Are you okay?" Lorrena asked. "Have you talked to my mother? Does she know what happened?"

Her grandmother shook her head. "Sit down, relax. We have so much to catch up on."

Lorrena stepped forward into her grandmother's slender arms. The woman squeezed her with force beyond her frail limbs. Gently pushing Lorrena back by the shoulders, her grandmother held Lorrena's face in her hands. Wrinkles filled the old woman's forehead as she peered over her glasses.

"Look at you! So many of your mother's traits, yet so monumentally different. You know, I've always seen you in my visions, but it's certainly not the same as having you right here in front of me."

Lorrena shrugged, searching for words.

"Don't look so bamboozled, my dear. Here are a few words of advice to you, since you're in shock, meeting your wild grandmother for the first time. You know, life is like one big puzzle if you don't look closely enough at the pieces you're given. But the pieces are with us always. We just have to learn how to put them together. Step back, and look at the whole story." She held up her pointer finger. "Oh, and write things down. That's important for you."

"I do write things down," Lorrena said. She put a hand in her pocket, empty aside from her lunch money and cell phone. She had left her journal in her room. "I didn't even know you existed until before we moved," she continued. "Not once did my mother mention you, not even as a kid when I asked where my grandparents were."

"Yeah, and you know it takes a lot to keep your mother silent," her grandmother said, chuckling. She pointed to the food tray. "Here, Lorrena. Eat this. I know when you're hungry it's harder for important information to sink in."

Lorrena grabbed the tray and settled in the small armchair beside her grandmother's bed. As she shoveled the eggs into her mouth, pieces spilled down her chin. She wiped the napkin across her mouth and looked up, smiling.

"Your mother means well. She cares about you. When she's yelling, that means she's especially concerned. But that's the thing about Erin. She doesn't know how to deal with affection. Instead she turns everything into a fight in order to keep her control."

"That's for sure," Lorrena said. "So what happened? Why doesn't she want to see you?"

"I haven't seen your mother in over twenty years. She ran away with your father to get married and never came back, until now. Adult Protective Services called her after I broke my hip. They helped me move in here. Erin ignored my phone calls for a few days, until I finally left her a message saying I might be dying. Twenty-five years, and we've talked for all of ten minutes."

Lorrena jumped to her feet. "You might *what?*"

Her grandmother tossed her hand in the air. "Settle down, child. Look at me! I'm more alive in this moment than ever before!" She shifted the blankets over her legs. "We all have our time to go, Lorrena. Remember that. I've certainly got more business to clear up before I leave, especially since I don't want to come back here for a while," she said, rolling her eyes. "Karma."

"So how'd you get her to move?" Lorrena asked.

Her grandmother smiled. "I told her the only thing I wanted was to spend time with my granddaughter. That I deserved it, even if she didn't speak another word to me."

"And she agreed? Just like that?"

"Goodness gracious, no! You know your mother. We

fought for a good five minutes before she agreed to take the house. She loved that house. Lived there all her life. If there's anything a person can't let go of, it's good 'ol childhood nostalgia. Not to mention, my intuition told me it would sell her."

Lorrena's insides churned. "But my dad built our house. How could she let go of that so easily?"

"When she must, Erin can shut down her emotions like that." Her grandmother snapped her fingers. "The day her dog got hit by a car when she was fifteen? She ran down the street to the ice cream shop and ate three whole ice cream cones. Deep down, she was aching. Where do you think her irritation stems from?"

"I don't know," Lorrena said. "I always thought she was angry that Dad died too, leaving us alone. I was only five and she yelled at me when I saw…" Lorrena's voice trailed off as her grandmother raised her head toward the ceiling and closed her eyes. Popping them open a minute later, her grandmother spoke in a distant tone.

"Your dad's house won't sell. Your mother rejected three offers already." She stared at the wall beyond Lorrena.

"What? How did you—" Lorrena stopped herself.

Her grandmother's focus remained distant for several minutes, without moving. Abruptly, she turned her head to meet Lorrena's gaze. "You know, I still remember the last thing she told me before she ran away with your father. 'I love you,' she said, 'but I hate the way you are.'" Her grandmother laughed, shaking her head. "Can you believe it? The way I am, like there's something wrong with it! You know, some things in life we have no control over. Sometimes all we can do is trust that we're being guided in the right direction, learn as best we can from the obstacles placed in our way by others, and through all the craziness, we must continue to put out good, positive energy. Basically, when your mother ran away, it was beyond any power that I had to bring her back. Until she learned to handle her hatred on her own."

"But why couldn't you find her?" Lorrena asked. "You're her mother. She never called or wanted to come home?"

"I knew exactly where she was, Lorrena. Just like, after a while, you knew where to find me. But do you see how long it took you to finally get here? Sometimes the harder we try to make things work, the more resistance we encounter. Everything has a way of sorting itself out, in time, so long as we remain optimistic with all of our heart. She was nineteen then. An adult, capable of managing her own life. Living in Connecticut with the love of her life, she didn't need me. That was her plan. She wanted to stay far away from me."

"She won't talk about it," Lorrena said. "Not even a word. But I still don't understand why she hated you so much."

"She hated that I wasn't normal. Whatever that is. She wanted a normal mother, like her friends. Around the house and such, I used my clairvoyance. I talked to people who'd passed away, channeled spirits, helped ghosts who didn't realize they were dead cross over to the Other Side. All of it mortified her. She was ashamed of me, especially since I taught English at her school. When rumors spread about my gifts, she hated me all the more. Then she met your father, and realized it was her chance to escape." Her grandmother paused. "Your mother kept you away from me to protect you, Lorrena. Little did she know, she was shielding you from the one person who'd really understand you."

Lorrena lowered her head. "But I don't want to see ghosts or hear voices. They attack my mind and I wish they'd just go away. I want friends too, and I don't want them to think I'm weird, and I want my mother to be happy."

Her grandmother's tone grew sharp. "You have a gift, Lorrena. It's part of you. If you deny it, you only make things harder on yourself. Besides, you already wrote it into the story of your life. To learn from it."

For a minute, Lorrena was silent. That young man's face popped into her mind. The way his mouth moved as if he were trying to tell her something. "What do I have to do?" she asked.

Her grandmother cleared her throat. "Listen closely, because this is very important for you."

Lorrena uncrossed her legs, leaning forward eagerly in her chair. Her grandmother looked her straight in the eye, her stare burning into Lorrena's. She could feel the power of the words released from grandmother's mouth.

"Clairvoyance, clairaudience. You see and hear things that exist at a higher vibrational frequency than the physical world we inhabit. These functions remain dormant in many people, although everyone has the ability to heighten their intuition and their psychic modalities with practice. Basically, your brain allows you to tap into this elevated frequency, as well as the alternate planes that merely overlay our own world. Like the Other Side, for instance, where time and space do not exist. When we 'die'," her grandmother explained, holding up quotation marks with her fingers, "we follow the beautiful, loving white light leading us to another dimension layered upon this one. Not way up in the clouds. Not buried under the ground in some fiery pit, but right here, around us. Within us." Her grandmother reached her arms outward, then folded them slowly back in again. "Sometimes in the process of leaving Earth, a soul will get lost for whatever reason. They get stuck, wandering between planes. People besieged by their own selfishness, and who refuse to discard their troubles and material

110

possessions. That's where you come in. Your job is to lead them into the light. Remind they're no longer alive in an earthly sense and that utter indescribable joy awaits them, if they so choose. Excuse me." Her grandmother released a cough.

"What about my father? Does he know I feel him around me?"

"Keep listening, child, I'm not finished. Most people, like your father for example, pass over effortlessly into the light. These spirits contact us simply to let us know they're okay. It is then, my dear, that you act as a medium for those who may not know that our loved ones exist all around us, whispering in our ears, pulling gently on our hair, filling the air with their scents, slipping simple objects from one place to another, traveling with us in our dreams. Endlessly reminding us they're alive and well, thriving beyond the mortal bodies they've shed. Yet the communication is never solid or concrete. How can it be, when our essences are not? Naturally, the human brain will rationalize. To find any sort of scientific explanation. You, Lorrena Shaw, have the power to override that rationalization. To translate the unknown into a language people will not be able to deny."

Lorrena sighed in frustration. "All I hear are jumbled voices that I can't tell apart. When I'm trying to sleep, or when I'm around people who'll think I'm crazy for hearing things."

"Then concentrate. If you don't want to hear anything, ask for silence. Filter the voices you know are important. When you see ghosts wandering around, guide them. And if a spirit wants you to relay a specific message, do it."

"The guy I've seen around the woman here in the nursing home. If I can remember what his name is…" Lorrena paused, searching through her memory banks without success. "Tell me, Gram, what does he want?"

A smile washed over her grandmother's face. "Ask him. I can't tell you everything and I've already said enough. You've got to see for yourself. It is the best way to truly learn. From experience, child."

"But I want to know right now."

"My dear, I must rest my voice. I'm tired and my aging eyes are heavy. Hold my hand. Push the voices away and listen to the sound of the particles bouncing off each other in the atmosphere."

Lorrena took her grandmother's warm, wrinkled hand in her own. The old woman's eyes shut, her lids quivering. As her breathing deepened, Lorrena knew her grandmother was asleep.

Lorrena too closed her eyes, allowing this new information to settle in her brain. As it did so, she thought again of the young man's image glowing in front of her eyes and soon it was no longer her grandmother's hand she was holding, but his, pulling her from her body into a bubble of light.

"Will I remember this when I wake up?" Lorrena asked him as they ascended upward.

"Tell yourself that you can, and you will. You must remember if you're going to carry through with your plan," James said.

They appeared in the same colossal library they had traveled to a few nights before.

"I don't want to read your book again," she said, recalling the fall from the motorcycle.

"You don't have to," he said. "Not now, anyway. This is my mother's book. She wrote you in here as a significant character, no matter how negatively she reacts to you."

"What do you mean?"

"See for yourself," he said, holding out the book.

Lorrena took the book in her hands. Though it was thickly bound, it felt weightless. As she plummeted through the pages, she appeared in the nursing home, looking into the lobby from a smaller room attached to it. Papers flew in every direction before settling onto the floor.

Lorrena's eyes shot open at the loud sound of knocking. She blinked. She was back in the green chair beside her grandmother's bed.

A woman opened the door, peeking her head inside. "Oh, I'm sorry, I didn't realize you two were still sleeping!"

"Mrs. Marietta, do come in," her grandmother said. "We were just waking up. I'd like to introduce to you my grand-daughter, Lorrena."

"Nice to meet you, Lorrena," Mrs. Marietta said. "You've been asleep for a while, Mrs. Gedolewen. I came in during lunchtime but didn't have the heart to wake you. It's almost two o'clock now, and we're gathering in the Recreation room for a game of Bridge. Are you interested to join us or would you like me to send in an attendant for you?"

"Almost two?" Lorrena stood, fixing her hair. "I have to go, Gram. My mother's expecting me home any minute. I can't be late. I don't want her to—"

"Calm down, my dear, it's okay. Run along. Come back and visit as soon as you can."

Lorrena embraced her grandmother.

"It was so lovely to see you again," her grandmother said, winking.

Lorrena smiled. "Of course." Waving, she hurried out the door and down the long hallway. As she rushed into the lobby, she nearly knocked into a woman standing in front of the door. "Oh, excuse me, I'm sorry," Lorrena said, not realizing until she looked back that it was the same woman she'd seen the night before.

Above her, a ball of light formed. Lorrena turned before it manifested into the figure of the young man. *James*, she thought, yanking her cell phone from her pocket. The clock read twelve past two: the exact time she'd be leaving school to return home. As Lorrena walked away, the voices in her mind reverberated in the distance.

CHAPTER TEN

"The nearest Dream recedes – unrealized –
The Heaven we chase–"
– Emily Dickinson

Jimmy Pollaski

I awaken to the sound of a pleasant melody lingering in a soft, warm breeze. I'm lying in a bed of glowing yellow flowers, wrapped in a blanket of green leaves—a cocoon of powerful energy cleansing me of my negative vibes. Lifting my head slowly, I feel as though I have been sleeping for decades. My soul rejuvenated, I bounce to a stand. The leaves encompassing my being disappear. I have shed the weight of twenty-five years of worry, stress, pain, and strain. Now I am free.

Two half-moon trellises guard the garden, ivy weaving

through their crevices.

Warmth touches my back and Dezba is beside me, surrounded by a thick aura of deep blue light. The singing grows louder in the distance.

"How do you feel?" she asks.

"Extraordinary," I say. "There is nothing like a long rest to restore my soul energy after my difficult departure from Earth. It was not at all how I pictured it, after many years of imagining."

Dezba smiles. "Of course not, although the imagination is a powerful thing. Often we do not realize that the truth lies in our thoughts, within the folds of our imagination, pushing the unbelievable into reality." Dezba cups her hands together. When she opens them, out flies a radiant fairy, buzzing around my ears. Its wings beat as fast as a hummingbird, its tiny body dressed in miniature pink gown. I grin, watching the fairy hover over my shoulder before it vanishes in a small explosion of light.

I take a few steps forward, and we move from the garden into an outdoor concert venue with a small stage. Green grass stretches out below the theater. There are many souls lying down, while others eagerly gather in a crowd at the foot of the stage. Small children are running around them, chasing after each other in fits of giggles.

"Ah yes, now I recognize the extreme splendor of the angels' songs," I say, looking up. The enormous white-bodied figures dance across the platform, their wings sparkling. Their soothing melody floats in the air, lifting my spirit. The experience emanates beauty beyond words, the perfection of the notes like nothing I have ever heard on Earth. The elegant chords of a harp resonate through the arena, accompanied by a round of piano.

Dezba twists into the air, flying. I look over my shoulder and notice Josephine dancing at my side. She takes my hand and twirls me in circles, and we too are lifting off of the ground. When I stop spinning, I see Emily and Grandpa Paul waltz by, into a large ceramic pot of white roses. Their bare feet pounce over the flowers without detaching a petal.

As Dezba lands, a beautiful golden violin appears on her arm. Breaking out in song, several other souls look in our direction and begin to dance with us. Everyone in the circle unites as if we are holding hands. It is not our hands which unite us though; it is our energy that locks together.

Even though the music continues to play, the scenes around us transform. Still secured in our circle, we appear in a thick jungle surrounded by towering palm trees and fern like giant feathers. A glistening waterfall drops into a giant lake, seemingly two hundred feet below, but I know this distance is a misconception. Bright pink orchids line the waterbed, and lily pads dot the deep blue water.

The elegant voices of the angels fade. I do not want them to stop, but their songs are replaced by tree frogs resting on the lily pads. A red and green parrot in a nearby tree calls out, triggering the tune of more birds hiding in the lush vegetation.

Dezba speaks. "James, we have taken a trip to a famous jungle spot, where incarnated souls often come when they dream. It is also a place where discarnate souls relax and practice dream adaptation techniques. Learning how to create and manipulate dreams of the living is an activity you were working on before you left for your life as Jimmy Pollaski. Your mother returns almost every night because her soul memory knows she will find you here. Whether you can get her to remember her dreams clearly when she wakes up will depend upon your skill level and practice."

"Yes," I say. "I remember doing this many times with my mother before I was born, although I must not have been the best at it then because she was continually imagining me as a girl!" I laugh.

I notice everyone in the circle has gone into a meditative state, manipulating their energy to match the vibrational frequency of their dreaming loved ones.

Allowing myself to sink into the center of my energy body—an action similar to closing my eyes on Earth—I can see my mother tossing and turning in her bed, though she is asleep. It is two o'clock in the morning Earth time, and I know she drifted off only an hour ago. She fears that her dreams will turn into ravaging nightmares, tearing her from her precious sleep. It is a constant struggle since she is afraid of both wakefulness and slumber. I feel the negative bursts of thought traveling through her brain, breaking apart her strong, blissful energy. Soon I will try to calm her mind by sending waves of energy particles to stimulate her optimism.

Right now she is dreaming of pushing a shopping cart filled with bags of heavy dirt around her house. I do not want to interrupt this dream for fear that she will interpret my message in the wrong manner, and so I must wait until she enters a dream taking place in this beautiful backdrop.

Finally, I hear my mother laughing. The image in her mind looks exactly like the jungle we are in now, except she is further back from the waterfall, picking a bouquet of orchids. Everyone in our circle has disappeared.

My mother selects a purple-speckled orchid and places it in her hair, admiring her reflection in the stream leading to the waterfall. Very carefully I project myself next to the thin trunk of the palm tree behind her. As I do so, my image reflects near hers and she gasps, more excited than scared.

"Jimmy," she says, spinning around, "you're okay."

"Mom, of course I am. You know that."

"I know. It is just so hard, not hearing your voice with my own ears. It's hard to believe it's real."

"You hear me now, Mom. Trust it." I take her hand, squeezing it three times like I used to do as a boy.

"It is definitely you, that's for sure. But you'll disappear with my dream, and I won't remember." My mother leans forward to add a few more orchids to her collection. She takes in a long, deep breath through her nose, admiring the magnificent scent of perfect flowers. "Sometimes I wish I could stay here with you forever. Never leave."

"Remember that a part of your energy remains here, even with your other half incarnated in your body. We are always together," I tell her.

"But it's not the same, Jimmy, not like it used to be. I want to take it all back, do it over again, and have you with us for dinner every night. See you get married, and watch your kids with Denise's, running around the yard. Just like I imagined it to be."

"Things are not always as we imagine, Mom. And sometimes they are more amazing than we ever could have expected!"

"How can I look forward to a future without you in it? How can it be amazing without you?"

She is regressing. I can feel her negative impulses working against my efforts. It is her guilt surrounding my death that triggers them. Lost hope of fading dreams. With her subconscious fears taking over, although I want so badly right now to calm her aching mind, I know it is a lesson she ultimately seeks to learn in her own time. My help in this moment is of little use.

I must let her go, for now. As I close my eyes, she does the same.

"Can't let go," she says, falling to her knees. The orchids drop to the ground, her bouquet scattering.

I place my hand on her back, sending her waves of my most vibrant, affectionate energy. "I love you, Mom."

The others in my group are exiting from their trance states. They appear around my mother but do not seem to be aware of her presence. I am half in my mother's dream, half in the spirit world.

"Come, Jimmy," a voice behind me says. "We're going for a ride down the waterfall!"

Dezba appears, signaling for me to follow her through the river. The water is warm against my spirit body, but it does not truly feel wet, a sensation I am not sure I can entirely describe with words. It is similar to waves of pleasant radiation rippling through me. The others ahead of me are approaching the drop-off of the waterfall. I watch them jump and hear the rush of the water, their cheers ringing out.

A light wind blows, catching the orchids and yanking them toward the rim of the cliff. My mother stumbles, reaches out her hands to catch them. Her figure is fading. Is her body almost awake?

"Jimmy, don't leave," she pleads, kneeling beside the stream just before it falls into the lake. The current has pulled away all of the orchids except for one. She is holding the light yellow flower in her hand, which she releases as she reaches for me.

"Rest, Mom. Everything will be okay," I promise. As I hold out my hand, I am surprised when she catches it. Her grip feels so real. Secure. The unmistakable feeling of physical contact.

Dezba follows the others down the waterfall, their beings disappearing into the mist. Laughter echoes throughout the canyon.

"Soon, Mom. I'll talk to you soon." Hanging on by the tips of her fingers, I look up into her face. Her eyes fill with worry. She appears to be holding on with all of her might, though I am weightless. I squeeze her hand three final times, and let go. Her image disappears as I slip over the side of the precipice.

Descending with the flow of the waterfall, I feel a surge of vitality. Then, I am no longer falling, but have merged with the droplets of water; the representation of my body transforms into a ball of yellow light, shimmering as light reflects off water.

When I reach the lake, the other souls also appear as spheres of illumination, brightening as they bathe in the lagoon of powerful vivacity. It is like we are swimming, though we do not have arms to paddle, nor do we need air to breathe beneath the water's surface. I am gliding deeper.

Dezba's blue light shines beside me, and I feel her listening.

"I failed," I say. "If she remembers this dream it will appear to her like a nightmare."

"You are learning," Dezba corrects. "We are always growing, especially in this dimension where knowledge is unlimited. Where fear, worry, hatred, evil—all created by the human ego—are not present. Failure, Jimmy, does not exist, because the wheel of life is always spinning. We always have another chance to change, and expand."

"Yes, yes, I know. I must practice, and I will be better at dream adaptation in no time. But for now, I will simply watch people's dreams, and not interfere until I know it is the perfect time."

Sinking into my energy body, I see my mother tossing and turning in her bed. Then I see Lorrena clutching her pillow, dreaming of her mother standing on the walkway of the nursing home while her grandmother hides in the bushes.

Abruptly, the image shifts again. Now I see a boy lying in a hospital bed. He has just awoken as the sun seeps through the opening in the blinds. Holding his hands over his chest, he smiles.

His hair is golden blond, like mine once was; his deep brown eyes glimmer with recognition. "Dream come true," he murmurs and nods off again, his hand still pressed against his body.

CHAPTER ELEVEN

Patricia Pollaski

Friday -- February 27th -- 4:38 a.m.

P atricia sat up fast, her heart pounding. She wiped the beads of sweat dripping down her forehead before tossing the bottom corner of the comforter from her upper body. Pulling the sheet up over her shoulders, she settled her head back down on the pillow.

It was the same reoccurring nightmare that woke her almost every other night—attempting to save Jimmy from falling into the raging waters hundreds of feet below. Every time, she let him plummet, unable to pull him up to safety, no matter how hard she tried.

Patricia stared at the back of her husband's head as he slept soundly curled up on his side, oblivious to her problems.

She wondered if the dream would ever turn out for the better. If one night, she would indeed rescue him. Sometimes after she woke up she would try to erase the last part of the dream, alter it so that she fell down into the ocean with him. Together they would be picked up by a giant yacht with an orange life raft, towing them to the safety. It was not the same. Even half awake, she was always aware that Jimmy was truly gone, and there was nothing she could do to save him.

Patricia closed her eyes tight, waiting for sleep to find her.

The image of Jimmy replayed over again until she tried hard to empty her mind, to imagine nothingness. She began to count backward from one hundred.

Ninety-nine, ninety-eight, ninety seven…

Finally, barely reaching the mid-seventies, she drifted off into a calm, dreamless sleep.

--7:59 a.m.--

Patricia breathed in the warm, fresh air through her nose. The morning was overcast, yet even with the clouds covering the sun as it rose behind them in the sky, the air felt like spring, unusual for February days in New England. Patricia pulled Anna by the hand down the nursing home walkway. The girl stumbled, dragging her feet as she walked.

"Let's go, Anna. Grammy's late for work this morning. Please cooperate."

"But I don't wanna go to work, Grammy P," she said, hanging her head.

"It'll be fun," Patricia said. "You play with your toys all

day anyway, it's not like you know what work is," she added under breath. Patricia dropped Anna's hand and held the door open for her granddaughter. The little girl shuffled through. Following behind her, Patricia looked up to find Mrs. Marietta closing the dining room's sliding stained-glass doors.

"Oh good, just who I wanted to see," Mrs. Marietta said, eying the little girl. "Would you mind filing some paperwork for me today instead of attending to residents? That way, she can play on the couch or something. No stress." Mrs. Marietta smiled.

"Sure," Patricia said.

"Great. Most of the patients are in the dining room eating breakfast anyway, so since you're taking over in the office, I'll go back to playing waitress." With a wink, Mrs. Marietta disappeared behind the stained glass.

Patricia stood without moving, exhausted from yet another sleepless night. Anna pulled on her pant leg.

"Grammy, I wanna have a tea party with Misses Miriam."

"Not now, Anna. Please go on the couch and take a nap."

"But I don't wanna take a nap. I wanna dip my cookies in tea and tell stories and dance."

Patricia picked up her granddaughter from under her arms and sat her down onto the small couch in the right corner of the office. "Play, then" she instructed.

Walking around the desk, Patricia dropped into the rolling chair, leaning her elbows on top of the paperwork, her chin on her hands. She watched Anna struggle to pull something out of her pocket. Finally, she released a Supergirl figurine. Pretending to fly it through the air, she waved her arms around, adding sound effects as she flung herself onto her back. Forgetting all about her surroundings, she shouted at her toys. "This way, Supergirl! Save the boy from the monster, ahh!"

Without looking at her work, Patricia watched her grand-daughter for what seemed like hours. Leaning back in the chair, she glanced at the clock, then at the stack of papers as the bell in the nursing home entranceway rang. She peaked around the doorway to find the girl who had run into her the day before, gradually making her way across the lobby. For a moment, the girl hesitated in her tracks, turned her head away, and back again. When Patricia caught her eye, the girl stepped into the office.

"Can I help you?" Patricia asked without standing.

"My grandmother…Miriam…I wanted to…" The girl looked down at her feet.

Anna stopped her figurines and raised her eyes, curious. "Misses Miriam?"

"Would you like to visit with Mrs. Gedolewen?" Patricia asked.

"No, um—yes. I will. I wanted to tell you. I mean—he does. Your son. He wanted me to tell you that he's okay."

"Excuse me?" Patricia frowned, unsure of whether she had heard correctly. Her hands trembled. She moved them around in search of the nearest solid object to hold on to, her left hand finding solace at the edge of the desk. The girl's eyes darted from Patricia's, upward, as if she were talking to the ceiling.

"Your son wants you to know that he's okay, so you can be happy again. So you can move on with your life," she said.

Patricia's heart pounded faster in her chest. She felt the tears welling up in her eyes, which she briskly wiped away. "My son is not alive anymore and he is most certainly not okay," Patricia said, her voice quivering.

Even as Patricia moved forward, the girl did not back away.

"But he's here in spirit, alive and well, Mrs. Pollaski, even though you can't see him. He watches you. He says if you can take comfort in that, you can be content, knowing you'll see him again, in time."

"How do you know my name? Get out of here before I call the manager!" Patricia yelled, pointing at the door. "My son is dead. I won't ever see him again." Patricia let the tears drop from her eyes, forming wet marks on the papers beneath her hand.

"I don't know what this means, but he says he will live on in the letter. He will find some way to write."

"Go!"

The girl flinched, edging backward until Patricia swept her arm across the desk, hurling the papers into the air. Manila folders fell open as the excess papers fluttered up, taking their time before scattering across the floor. Patricia watched as Anna slid from the couch to her feet, eyes wide.

The mysterious girl turned and ran out. Patricia stepped toward her granddaughter, dropping to her knees as she sobbed into the small girl's shoulder. "I'm so sorry. I'm so, so sorry," she said. She picked Anna up into her arms, rocking her back and forth.

"It's okay, Grammy P," Anna said, "Don't cry."

"Patricia, are you all right?" Mrs. Marietta rushed to her side. "My gosh, what happened? I heard screaming and—did someone try to break in? Are you hurt? What in the world happened?"

Patricia's words shook. "I don't...there was a girl and...my son." Patricia began to cry at full force, powerless to restrain the tears spilling from her eyes. The pain in her chest intensified. She couldn't understand how it felt as though her heart were splitting in two—hearts did not really break. Yet the more she cried, the better it felt, and she could not stop.

"Breathe, for goodness' sake," Mrs. Marietta said, rubbing Patricia's back. Patricia tried to collect her composure. Although her tears had stopped, she shuddered uncontrollably as she spoke, the sobs burning her lungs. "It was...I don't know. Mrs. Gedolewen's granddaughter. Said she could talk to my son. I just...don't know anymore." She wiped her face with her hands, and kept them there as she waited for her breathing to normalize. Finally, she took a gasp full of air, releasing it gradually through her nose. The heaviness subsided only for a moment.

"Why don't you run to the bathroom? Wash your face with some cold water," Mrs. Marietta said.

"Sure," Patricia replied. "Anna, you stay here. Grammy P. will be right back, okay? Play with Supergirl for a little while."

Patricia rushed to the lobby bathroom, locking the large single stall behind her. Peering into the mirror, a red-eyed, puffy-faced woman stared back, a woman she hardly recognized—blue bags weighing down her eyes, blonde hair graying at the roots, tiny creases at the outer corners of where her lids met. As she blinked, this woman blinked, and as she stared, this woman's pupils constricted, but as she took in the familiar face in its entirety, she had a difficult time believing it was her looking out from behind those eyes. Who had she become? Although she followed along with each of the motions this woman underwent, she wondered if there wasn't perhaps more to her beyond these actions, a substance that felt, saw, and understood, without the use of her eyes. The more the girl's words replayed in her head, the less she feared them. *He's here in spirit, alive and well, even though you can't see him*. The idea set a part of her at ease, no matter the apparent impossibility. When she thought about it, life itself was overflowing with mysteries that possessed no concrete explanations, including the notion that at death, a person's mind may simply go blank. How could she know for sure? What would the point of living be, she wondered, if everything in the end was lost? The thoughts restored the nerves in her stomach, and so Patricia set them out of her mind.

Spinning the sink's silver knob, she watched the cold water pour out until she conjured up enough energy to lean her face forward into the water flowing from the faucet. Refreshing against her flushed cheeks, Patricia closed her eyes and let it run into her ears, down her neck, cleansing her of her irritation. Peering into the mirror again, dampness tugged at the pieces of her hair around her face. She ran her hands along her cheeks and breathed. She was alive. *Barely going, but still alive*, she thought.

Patricia turned and flicked out the lights before heading back into the office. Mrs. Marietta was already sorting papers from the floor as Anna handed them to her.

"Look, Grammy P, I'm a big girl and I'm helping cause I don't want you to be sad," Anna said.

"Thanks, Anna," Patricia said. She looked over at Mrs. Marietta. "You really don't need to do this. I made the mess. I should be the one cleaning it up."

"Well, there's always room for a third set of hands. Besides, you can re-sort it once we gather it all together."

"Great," Patricia said.

"The more important issue though, is if you're okay. If you want to talk about it, please don't hesitate."

Patricia fidgeted. For a moment she was quiet. She looked over at Anna who had stopped picking up papers to dance her figurine over a manila folder sprawled out on the floor. "I don't even know. This girl came in saying she could see my son. I've been so sensitive lately, not able to sleep. I dream about him every night, tormenting dreams that pull him into a black void and every time, I'm the one who lets him fall. I'd like so much to believe that he's okay, but I just—I don't know what to believe anymore. How is it fair that someone so young can be taken from the world so soon?" Patricia rubbed her eyes.

"And why do others live on until their bodies and their minds are dysfunctional, until they've forgotten who they are? Unable to tend to simple tasks they've conquered years on end?" Mrs. Marietta asked. "I've dealt with death for a long time now, Patricia. You have as well."

"I have," she agreed.

"Death is most certainly never fair or easy, no matter when it sneaks up. No matter its timing, it's a part of life everyone must deal with. No one is exempt. We have to accept it as it comes, and have confidence that after the storm, there's serenity. At least that's the way I try to look at it every day I leave here and return home to rest."

Patricia nodded. "Well, you'd think after working here for so long it'd be easier for me to accept, too. But after I lost my mother years ago—when it's someone you've imagined by your side forever, it's hard to be optimistic. Losing my son has thrown me over the edge. It's just not fair," Patricia said, her voice hardening. "How do I keep going when I feel as though I'm losing everything I care about and I can't do anything but watch it slip away? I could've stopped him from moving to California. I could've called him that morning. I could've given him more money to buy a car instead of letting him use that awful motorcycle. But I didn't. I just...I wish I didn't feel as though it were my fault. Like I could've done something differently. And my husband. He just doesn't under..." Patricia let the word drift off.

"Patricia, I know it's hard, but you can't blame yourself. That sort of guilt will surely weigh you down. There was nothing you could have done. I know that being a mother and all, you feel like it's your job to protect your children, no matter the circumstances. But if you think about it, our residents here were once children with their own family members who were lost along the way. The cycle goes on. There's no telling what can happen in any given situation, no matter a person's age."

Mrs. Marietta didn't look at Patricia, but kept her eyes drifting to the corner of the office. "I remember years back, there was one resident in particular," Mrs. Marietta said. "Gladis, her name was. She was not too old, in her early seventies maybe, but she had bone cancer spreading all the way up her legs. Couldn't walk, but refused to check into a hospital or get any treatment. Her daughter admitted her into Kendall Retirement because the old woman had friends here, and it was the only help she would accept. The worst part was that you could see the pain in Gladis' eyes growing stronger, but at the same time she'd wear a strange, distant smile. She'd look out at the dark New England sky and tell you that even though she could only see the clouds, the sun was always shining somewhere."

"Wow, that's crazy," Patricia said, raising her eyebrows.

"Keep listening, it gets crazier." Mrs. Marietta cleared her throat. "Her daughter and I would stand by the doorway talking with her until she'd fall asleep mid-sentence. Her daughter was so frustrated by the woman's stubbornness. She wanted so badly to ease her mother's pain, but the more she tried to convince her to take any sort of medication, the more Gladis was convinced she didn't need it. Every inch of pain she endured, Gladis said, the stronger she'd become in the end.

"One night her daughter and I were chatting just before going home to sleep. There was one light on, not too bright or anything, but all of a sudden the room lit up like the middle of the day. It was like nothing I had ever seen before. Nothing to justify it, no science to explain it—just a small golden ball of light drifting outward from the old woman's body. And you could feel in the air, the release of her pain as the light extended up before it disappeared, the room going dark again. It was one of the most intense experiences of my life."

"You saw it? Are you sure you hadn't fallen asleep too?"

"I was standing right there. I saw it with my own two eyes. We both did. And I'll tell you, it wasn't the last time it happened either."

"That's unbelievable. It sounds like a story that girl would tell," Patricia said with a nervous chuckle.

"If you don't mind my asking, what exactly did she say?"

Patricia hesitated. *Here in spirit, alive and well*, the words resonated in her mind. "She said she sees him around me, but honestly, I don't know how this teenager could know anything about what I'm going through. Talking to people who no one else can see? My son is dead. It's just not feasible, and I can't wrack my brain trying to make sense of it." Patricia snapped, her eyes again glassing over. She looked at Anna who stared up at the two women, sitting cross-legged on the floor with her Supergirl figurine propped upright against her knee.

"Grammy P, what's fee-spell mean?"

"Another day, Anna. Will you pass Grammy those folders near you?"

"Yes, Grammy P," Anna said, her tiny fingers prying the papers from the floor.

"I think I got it from here," Patricia said. She crouched down to gather the leftover documents. "I'll let you know if I get stuck sorting any of this out."

Mrs. Marietta smiled, patted Patricia's shoulder. "And I'll be back to make sure everything is okay."

"Thanks," Patricia said. As she righted the mess of papers, a name on the top paper caught her eye. Ms. Miriam Alice Gedolewen. Recent Injury Report: Hip fracture. Address: Moved from 86 Main Street. Insurance: HMO Blue. A shiver ran up her arms. Family status: No surviving members.

--1:38 p.m.--

Setting the final folder in alphabetic order, Patricia nudged the file cabinet closed with her hip. Looking up at the clock, she realized it had taken her several hours to arrange everything for the one second it'd taken to throw it around the room.

"No one's fault but my own," she muttered.

Anna waved her arms around, making her Supergirl figurine dive straight toward the floor. "Nope," the little girl said, swooping the doll up before it hit the ground.

Patricia shot a glance toward the entrance when the bell rang through the quiet lobby. Half expecting to see Lorrena come running in, Patricia was surprised when a woman who appeared to be in her early forties stuck her head through the doorway without completely entering. After a few moments, the woman stepped forward, closing the door slowly behind her. Her long dark hair swung around her face as she peered through the dining room's sliding glass doors. She was dressed in a black jacket, her dark blue jeans tucked into her boots.

Patricia stood, sliding the rolling chair into the desk before making her way into the lobby. The woman jumped.

"May I help you?" Patricia asked.

"I'm looking for someone."

"If you let me know their first and last name, I could look them up in the directory."

The woman spoke softly. "She's not a patient here. She's my daughter. I think she may be visiting someone."

Patricia eyed the woman. "Dark hair, blue eyes, wearing a green puffy jacket?"

"That's her."

"I have seen her. She should be in room 17. Mrs. Gedolewen's room," Patricia said.

"Yes. That's the one. Would you mind going to get her for me? I'm not exactly sure where that is." The woman's face remained expressionless. Her arms rested at her sides.

"Ma'am, it's right down that hall," Patricia said, pointing. "Very easy to find, but um, I'd be happy to escort you there, if that'd make you feel better?"

"I'm in a hurry. If you could send her along I'd really—"

"It's this way," Patricia said, waving her hand toward the corridor. She pulled the door handle, holding it open for the guest. The woman hesitated before reluctantly stepping forward. "It's funny, I was just looking at her file a few hours ago. I've been working with her a lot lately. Very nice lady."

"Yes," the woman said. "That is funny. I haven't seen her in a while."

Patricia gazed into the woman's face as her eyes darted away. An uncomfortable silence filled the air.

"Well, here it is. Room 17." Patricia opened the door without looking in. She waited for the woman to step in first, but she wouldn't budge. "After you."

"Sure."

Patricia followed behind her, and both women looked around in disbelief.

The room was empty.

CHAPTER
TWELVE

Lorrena Shaw

Friday -- February 27th -- 8:10 a.m.

Backpedaling into the lobby, Lorrena turned and stumbled through the double doors. She jogged down the hall to her grandmother's room without looking back. The woman's sobs sounded muffled through the walls. Lorrena stopped at the door, hesitating. Without knocking, she spun the doorknob. She assumed her grandmother would be lying in bed, waiting to enlighten her about the most recent turn of events. Instead of her grandmother's pale face lighting up the room, Lorrena found it to be empty. The wind yanked at the curtains, a temperate breeze circulating through the air. Despite its surprising warmth, goose bumps rose up over her arms. An overwhelming fear consumed her. What if her grandmother had passed away in her sleep? Otherwise, she would've seen in one of her visions that Lorrena would be there.

Lorrena's eyes darted across the room. The first bed was still stripped of its attire, yet her grandmother's blankets remained neatly spread over her bed without a wrinkle, the pillows perfectly propped up.

Lorrena crept around the far side of the bed, dropping her backpack onto the armchair. Pulling her journal from the front pocket, she climbed atop the blue covers, resting her back between a nook in the pillows. A strong scent of baby powder lingered in the air. James' image flashed through her mind. His representation intensified every time Lorrena saw him reaching out for his mother—who was completely unaware of his presence.

Lorrena slid the pen from the spiral binding and began writing. Her hand glided effortlessly across the page, the words pouring from her mind. *I remember wondering what it would feel like to die. How would I know when it happened?* After a few pages, she stopped. The door creaked open as an attendant wheeled her grandmother into the room. A look of surprise formed on the old woman's face.

"Oh, I'm so sorry, darling. I had no idea you were coming," her grandmother said. "Funny, my mind must finally be going."

"Please don't say that, Gram. It isn't funny. You're going to be okay," Lorrena said, closing her journal. She hopped off the bed and hurried to her grandmother's side.

The attendant smiled as she leaned over to adjust the wheelchair. "Who's this, Mrs. Gedolewen?"

"This is my granddaughter, Lorrena," the old woman said, proudly lifting her stiff shoulders.

"Oh, isn't that nice of her to visit. You don't have any school today, Lorrena?"

"No, not today," Lorrena said with a nervous laugh.

"Thank you for your help, Jean. Breakfast was nice today. I'll call you in later if I need you, but I think my granddaughter and I are visiting together this afternoon."

"All right, I'll give Mrs. Marietta the heads up. Let us know if you're stuck." With that, the attendant left.

"I thought you were gone," Lorrena said abruptly.

"Gone where, child? Can't get very far in this thing." Her grandmother winked as she tapped the wheels of her chair. She released a light wheeze laced with her laughter.

"I told the woman that I could see her son. He wanted me to send her the message, but she freaked out. I figured you'd be waiting for me like last time, to tell me how to use my gift if they won't listen. When you were gone, I thought surely that…"

"Calm yourself, and come here. Lift this lever behind the wheel. We're going for a walk and I will explain then."

"You mean, we're going outside?"

"Well, the scenery isn't too great inside the center, although the pictures of the Gloucester Harbor are lovely. I thought maybe we could walk to the beach, and experience it in its true form. It's been so long since I've felt the ocean breeze. Not to mention, it's important to take advantage of any warm New England day in February."

"But it's cloudy out, Gram."

"Don't argue with your elders. Let's go. Left toward that exit sign, in the opposite direction of the lobby."

Lorrena unlocked the wheel without further dispute. Maneuvering the chair out of the room, they headed toward the exit sign lit up in small red letters. She glanced down the other side of the hallway to make sure no one saw them. "They don't care if we leave, do they?"

"Of course not. This is a retirement center, not a jail," her grandmother assured. "The pass code is right under the key-pad. Put in the numbers and we're good to go."

Lorrena tapped the soft gray buttons, and the door clicked open. Out they went, under the thick cloud-cover which contradicted the pleasant breeze. She admired the way warm air packed her nose with substance, contrasting to the winter's cold, sharp winds, devoid of the sturdy elements she couldn't quite pinpoint.

The cement walkway guided them around the building before dumping them out beside the tall bushes outlining the parking lot.

"Follow this street here, Oceanridge Road," her grandmother said.

The road narrowed, bending around the houses to the right before winding down a small hill. Trees filled in the scenery, their jagged branches slicing into the sky.

"I can smell the salt in the air already," Lorrena said.

"Always a sign that the ocean is alive and well, not too far away."

"Like James," Lorrena said. "That's what he wanted to tell his mother."

"Ah, yes. What else has he said, child?"

"In my dreams, Gram, I vaguely remember him telling me about a book—a book that I'm going to write myself. I'm not sure if it's possible since I don't know the first thing about writing anything except in my journal. And I only write when I don't feel like doing my homework or cleaning my room. Besides, it's just a bunch of scribbles about my day."

"Ah, but you've written much more than you give yourself credit for. Look around. What do you see?"

"What do you mean?" Lorrena watched her feet move

over the bumpy pavement, the wheelchair rolling around pot-
holes in the road which had collected puddles. She waited for a
response from her grandmother.

"What do you see?" her grandmother repeated.

"Okay. Well, I see the trees, and the houses, and the road,
and soon I'll see the beach."

"Yes. You're moving, taking in new surroundings every
moment. But what you don't see are the forces that lead us in
different directions. You don't see the energy that drives us to
the places we go each day, like school, or work, or the nursing
home, when others think we should be elsewhere. You only
see the solid objects that define our paths, and our plan. The
plan that you wrote before your life began, detailing everything. Even this walk we're taking now."

Lorrena looked around at the trees swaying, the cottages
boarded up for a winter's rest. Seagulls screeched overhead.
"But what if I decide I don't want to continue on this walk?
Say I turn back?" she asked, her voice filled with wonder.
"There can't be a set fate, or we wouldn't have choices. I know
I have the power to turn us around so they don't yell at me for
stealing you away."

Her grandmother laughed. "You're right, my dear. We all
have free will. Many decisions divert us from our predisposed
path, invisibly etched within a book with no true binding, no
real pages that you can feel with your hands. But no matter
how far we may diverge from our path, eventually we will find
our way."

"A book," Lorrena said, the words sinking into her comprehension. In front of her, a plastic bag swooped toward the
road, halting in mid-air before the wind yanked it away, catching it on a branch. Lorrena's eyes followed past the top of the
tree to where the deep blue of the Atlantic extended into the

darkened sky. The crashing of the waves filled her ears. "What does this have to do with the book I'm going to write? I still don't understand."

"Our life plans are stored within the Akashic Records— records of every person in the Universe who has ever lived, and ever will live in the future, scrawled across the Ether— words constantly shifting and erasing. Rewriting and evolving until the present moment is cemented into the past," her grandmother said, shrugging. "Perhaps you'll simply put it to paper."

"How do I write the details of my life, let alone someone else's? How can I remember it all?"

"Listen to the voices, Lorrena. Separate the important ones from the nonsense and they will provide the insight you need to help you share your gift. Tell yourself every night before you fall asleep to remember your dreams clearly when you wake up, so you can write them down."

"Lucky for me, all I hear right now is the ocean."

The road twisted to an end. A stone wall, consisting of various sized rocks unevenly piled on top of one another, divided the sand from the street. A small inlet led to a path marked by flat stones cutting through the dunes to the soft, white sand. Waves pulled at the shoreline further down the beach. The strong smell of low tide danced under Lorrena's nose.

"Gram, we have to stop here. I don't think the wheelchair will go in the sand."

"Stop here? I don't think so," her grandmother said. "Carry me. I want to lie in the sand."

"Carry you? But I don't want to hurt you!"

"Look at me, Lorrena. I've shriveled down to a pile of skin and bones. It hurts being stuck in this wheelchair more

141

than anything else."

"I'll try," Lorrena said. She slid her arm carefully behind her grandmother's neck, securing a loose grip around her shoulder as her other arm hooked under the old woman's knees. To her surprise, her grandmother weighed no more than a heap of pillows.

Her grandmother rested her head against Lorrena's shoulder. "It's days like today I wish I had my vision back, to see the sky without it looking like a mess of fuzzy nothingness." Her silver hair brushed against Lorrena's face. She was not wearing her glasses.

Lorrena dodged clumps of seaweed, an empty crab shell crunching beneath her shoe. "But it's so cloudy and dark right now, Gram."

"I want to see the clouds moving a mile a minute like they're on a mission," her grandmother said, "and the sea so blue as the light shimmers through the waves. I want to see the crevices in the rocks again, and the seaweed swaying. The hermit crabs, stretching their red little legs until their eyeballs pop out of their shell, and the snails opening their black doors, with the mini shrimp jumping around them in the tide pools. All of the things your eyes lit up at when you were so small and attentive."

Lorrena took a few steps forward and immediately placed her grandmother into a velvety bed of sand. "Are you comfortable like this? Do you want me to put my jacket under you? I don't want the sand to get in your sweater."

Her grandmother's withered arms lay lifeless by her sides, her legs set out straight. Her off-white shoes dangled to each side as if they belonged to a puppet whose master had released their strings. Lorrena couldn't tell if her grandmother's eyes were opened or closed.

"I'm fine. I haven't felt this comfortable in twenty years. Now come, relax. Lie down next to me, and listen to the waves collapsing and reviving again. If you listen closely enough, you can hear little creatures scampering across the bottom of the seafloor."

Balancing both her feet on one of the rocks bordering the top of the beach, Lorrena looked out across the water, her hand propped up at her eyebrows. The ocean stretched out for miles without stopping. Seagulls perched on the rocks yelled to one another over the commotion of the waves. The sea-salt stuck to her skin.

"I'll try," Lorrena said. She bent down, sweeping her hand across the sand to even out the surface. Stretching out beside her grandmother, Lorrena laid her head back on a thick piece of driftwood. She admired the colors of the ocean. For a moment, she felt at peace. Soon after, her body's tranquility was broken after glancing worriedly at her grandmother to see if she was still breathing. It appeared as if she was not taking any air in at all. Lorrena watched, waiting for movement until she detected her grandmother's chest moving up and down slowly but steadily. If even for a minute it seemed that the progression had stopped, she would wait for her grandmother's stomach to round upward again to set her at ease.

When Lorrena saw a shadowy figure move out of the corner of her eye, she didn't say anything for fear that it would disrupt her grandmother's serenity. The figure took the shape of a man, hobbling over the rocks as he looked out to sea. He was dressed in a white sailor uniform with blue trim that was torn around the neck. Lorrena blinked and moments after, he disappeared.

"Are your eyes closed, Lorrena? You have to close them in order to tune into the workings of the Universe. Don't be

143

distracted by anything else."

"But I don't want to fall asleep, Gram, if the tide's coming up," Lorrena said. She watched the sailor ghost reappear. He floated a few feet above their heads, so close to Lorrena's face that she felt a burst of dampness over her skin.

Lorrena closed her eyes only for a moment, concentrating deeply on her inner-knowing. She felt that this man had gotten lost out at sea. "You love the sea so much you don't want to leave, huh," she said to the ghost.

The man gazed at her, deep sadness filling his eyes.

"It's okay," she said. "You can always come back to visit. Your wife and kids passed over years ago. They're waiting for you."

Just by looking at him, Lorrena learned that his name was Edwin McGarvey. His ship, the Night Watcher, had gotten lost in a dense fog in early 1855 and sunk after the bottom ripped apart on sharp rocks. Three days later, his body, along with several other crewmembers, had washed up to shore. His spirit had roamed the beachside ever since, too attached to his love for the ocean to leave it behind.

"Follow the light, Edwin," she said. "The light is always there to guide you."

The devastation in his eyes calmed, like the passing of a sudden storm. This time, as he watched the waves push in gently toward the beach, his head rose up slightly above the ocean to a bright white light that opened like a hoop on fire before him. Just like that, he disappeared.

"Beautiful," her grandmother said. "Very well done, Lorrena. Now, come. Clear your mind. You must do so if you want to fully recall the dreams significant to your writing."

Lorrena smiled, laying her head back down in the sand. "It's bizarre. I know I've been having crazy dreams, but I can't quite put my finger on them. It feels so real, flying away to far off places."

"Yes, Lorrena. Those dreams are real."

Lorrena shifted her body to the side. "But that doesn't make sense, Gram. If they're dreams, how are they real? How is flying possible?"

The wheezing in her grandmother's chest grew stronger. "Have you heard of astral travel, Lorrena?"

"No," she answered. "It sounds like some kind of space mission."

Her grandmother chuckled. "I guess you could look at it that way—or rather, a mission beyond space. It is when the soul separates safely from the body, soaring to wherever in the Universe it wants to go. Often times you travel through different astral planes, outside of what we call 'distance.' Just because you can't touch your soul, doesn't mean it's not real. Real is only a word we use to define concrete notions in the physical world."

"Really?" Lorrena asked, although in the pit of her stomach, she knew. Flashes of her dream arose—James taking her hand and pulling her from her bedroom, as if traveling through the depths of the solar system into the core of a star.

"Yes. Every person experiences it, almost every night. We just don't remember it. Astral travel is also one of the easiest ways to communicate with those who we've lost in physical form, without breaking the strict layer between life and death. When apart from the body, our Universal mind—the mind of our soul—recalls everything that's ever happened to us, or anyone else, if we choose to access it. When we wake up it's simply too much for our conscious mind to grasp, and so we push it from our reminiscence."

As her grandmother spoke, more elements of her dream

entered her mind. James held up the book. She saw the nursing home from his mother's point of view: a mirror image from the way Lorrena had seen it in real life. A strange feeling of déjà vu overcame her. "I remember part of my dream, Gram. It actually happened!" Lorrena sat up fast. "I was James' mother. I fell into her story's pages and today, when I gave her James' message, I experienced my dream from the opposite side of the room. He urged me to tell her that I could see him, but he knew she wouldn't listen."

Her grandmother grinned, her eyes still closed.

"What is it, Gram? Why are you smiling?"

"Write it down. It's the only way she'll believe you. Only when she sees her life from another person's eyes, will she take your gift seriously."

"I will," Lorrena said. "I'll write my own book of our books. James, Patricia, and I." Lorrena lay onto her back, gazing up at the clouds sweeping across the sky. Wound up from her recent revelation, she found it hard to sit still. Fidgeting her body into different positions, the sand trapped itself under her blue jeans as she pondered where she would begin her book. *The day I learned I could see ghosts and spirits? No, I'll begin the day I learned of my grandmother. Does it start there? Maybe it doesn't begin with my story at all.*

Lorrena remained quiet, listening to the words passing through her mind, and to the water lapping at the shore. After a while, she lifted her head as a raindrop spattered onto her nose. More raindrops hit her legs and her arms. "Gram, are you okay? It's starting to rain, and it's getting late. The school day ends soon. I don't want my mother to know I skipped."

Lorrena waited, listening.

"Gram? Gram, wake up. Are you okay?" Lorrena leaned over, placing her hand on her grandmother's arm. The fabric of her white sweater was damp from the rain.

The old woman's eyes still closed, she said, "I'm okay, my darling. I'm just thinking. Lost between this world and the next. The past and the moment leading into another, and another, until there are too many to count. You know how many I've lived through?"

"No, Gram."

"Eighty-two years. Billions of moments leading to this very moment. Here, on this beach. Do you know what it's like after eighty-two years of seeing things? Today I see—" Her grandmother stopped speaking.

"That's a lot. What does eighty-two years feel like, Gram?"

"A long, long time. Yet no time at all."

Lorrena stood, tilting her head up to the sky. She shut her eyes as the rain poured down harder, soaking her face. Water slid into her jacket, and her eyes popped open. Reaching into her pocket, she pulled out her cell phone. The screen displayed ten missed calls.

"Oh no, Gram. Mom's been calling. We have to get back to the nursing home quickly. What if she knows I skipped school? She's gonna be so mad."

Her grandmother struggled to lift her shoulders. Lorrena leaned down to pick her up. Her shoes stuck in the moistened sand as they stumbled back to the wheelchair together. After setting her down in the chair, Lorrena took off her jacket and draped it around her grandmother's body. She took one last glance at the ocean, where the rain sent tiny ripples across its compliant surface. Then she wheeled her grandmother forward.

"Your mother doesn't have the right to be mad at anyone. She's the one hiding from her problems. If anything, she's angry with herself."

"I'm pretty sure she's angry at the whole entire world," Lorrena said, rolling the wheelchair faster after dodging a pothole.

"She must learn to let her anger subside. It's vital to one's growth to exercise patience, forgiveness, and acceptance. To experience love and loss. It's important to use our time on Earth wisely; if we don't learn from the treacherous cycles of abuse and rage that surround humankind, similar experiences repeat in future lives until they're conquered. I've been waiting over twenty years to see your mother again."

"Do you wish you could've changed things so she wouldn't have left?"

"The past is only in our minds, Lorrena. We can't ever get the moments back, so why dwell on them? We only have right now. Reflect, and move on."

Lorrena glanced behind her. The beach had already disappeared out of view. "Why don't you tell her that? I'll drag her to the nursing home if I have to."

"If I could see her again, I'd tell her that I love her no matter how foolishly she acted for so many years. But—"

"But what? Why don't you?"

"I don't know if I'll have the chance in this life. I feel like…"

The nursing home emerged from behind the trees. "Like what, Gram? What do you see?"

"Nothing," she said. "I see nothing."

Lorrena frowned. "Well, I won't have the chance to tell her either considering she'll probably kill me when she finds out I skipped school."

Just as the words escaped Lorrena's lips, James' mother came running around the bushes, out of breath. Her eyebrows bent inward, her lips pursed.

"Mrs. Gedolewen! Are you okay? Let's get you inside. It's awful out here. We don't want you to catch anything."

"Yes, Patricia. I'm fine," Mrs. Gedolewen said.

Patricia eyed Lorrena, taking the wheelchair handles from her grip. They continued down the street, the nursing home just up ahead.

"I warned her that it was not a nice day to take a walk, regardless of the warm temperature. But she insisted," Lorrena said.

"Oh, hush." Her grandmother held her palms up. "Everyone needs a little rain once in a while, especially people like me who are cooped up in a building."

Lorrena followed close behind Patricia as they made their way down the walkway. Her bright yellow poncho rapped against the wheelchair as she walked.

"Have you been looking for us long?" Lorrena asked.

"For a little while. At least since—" Patricia stopped when Lorrena's mother pushed her way through the door. Water poured from the gutters spattering onto her clothes. She stood without moving, holding the door open with her shoulder.

"Erin," Mrs. Gedolewen said.

"Miriam."

"Mother. Call me Mother." Mrs. Gedolewen's voice cracked through her wheezing.

"Mother," Erin repeated. "It's been so long. I'd forgotten that I had one."

"Well, you do. You always have."

Patricia slowly rolled the wheelchair forward. "I'm sorry to interrupt, but we should probably get you inside, Mrs. Gedolewen. We don't want you to get sick."

149

Erin stumbled back, leaving the door in Lorrena's hands. Lorrena shook her head, anticipating her mother's typical outburst. Her grandmother's wheelchair stopped a few feet in front of her mother in the middle of the lobby. Yet instead of an angry rant, Erin's response was soft and withdrawn.

"I'm sorry. I didn't mean to be away for so many years. It's just the way it happened. I was trying to protect Lorrena."

"Protect her from what? From herself? She has a gift, Erin. No matter if I'm around to implement it," the old woman said sternly. "You cannot deny it because it will always come back to haunt you. Literally."

Lorrena coughed, the noise reverberating through the lobby. She realized after another cough sounded that it was coming from a small girl sitting cross-legged beside her feet. The girl looked up, her little gray eyes wide with anticipation as if she understood the urgency of the meeting between the adults.

"I left because I wanted a normal life, without all of your hocus pocus."

"And is that what you got? Sometimes the very thing we want is the one thing we can never have."

Lorrena turned in the direction of the door as a bell rung above her head. A woman rushed in, water dripping from her hair. "Man, it's awful out there," she said to Patricia as she shook out her jacket. "You know the temperature's supposed to drop thirty degrees tonight and all this rain's turning to snow?"

Lorrena looked at the woman for a minute before realizing it was her homeroom teacher who she'd met briefly the previous day.

The small girl jumped up, clapping her hands. "Mommy!"

"Anna! I'm here early today, honey. They let me go before after-school hours just for you." The woman bent down to pick up her daughter, kissing her on the cheek. She looked into the little girl's face with a smile, tucking her curls behind her ears. She scanned the faces in the lobby, the grin from her face slowly fading. "Mom, is everything okay?"

Patricia shook her head. "Yes, Denise. I think…everything will be fine."

Lorrena watched her teacher. As she did so, James' image resurfaced as it had the previous morning. Her arms tingled. She felt his presence stronger than ever before. A magnificent light blazed throughout the room, filling her with warmth. Her grandmother sat motionless, her eyes fixed on Erin. Lorrena's mother watched the floor. Her head lifted as Lorrena spoke.

"He is here right now." The words came from deep within her chest. "He wants to assure you that he's around you every day. Not in the way that is most satisfying, but he will brush your hair over your shoulder or shift objects in the slightest manner. He'll move your alarm clock, or open windows, or send feathered friends to say hello for him."

Lorrena closed her eyes, pausing for a moment to listen. She couldn't hear voices speaking to her—it was as if the radio in her mind had turned off. Instead the words pushed up into her throat. He was speaking through her, manipulating her vocal chords. When she opened her eyes, the light was gone. Yet Jimmy's presence remained, a strong, brilliant energy overtaking the room. Lorrena waited for someone to protest. Nothing could be heard but the sound of rain pounding on the roof, drowning out the hushed weeping of the women who stood in a loop around Lorrena.

Patricia lifted her right hand to wipe her tears, Denise a mirror of her image as her left hand moved across her cheek. Even after a lifetime of being apart, Lorrena's mother and grandmother also possessed this odd parallel. Erin's eyes squinted and opened wider in the same manner as Miriam's, releasing silent tears. Lorrena realized then, as each woman cried for a different reason, that there was something implicit about family members uniting with each other. Perhaps it was the idea that relatives were supposed to remain by one's side, their presence never questioned. Family members were the people who were never supposed to abandon you, no matter what the circumstance.

Lorrena cleared her throat as more of James' words manifested from within her. "He knows this sounds strange, but he wants you to be happy for him. He's sorry he had to leave so soon. He doesn't want you to halt your own life for him, though. Cry, but keep going. Grieve, but eventually let your sadness go. He is in a beautiful, loving place with Nonna, and Emily, and the others. He wants you to know he was around at the hospital—he was trying to wave to you, no matter what the doctors said. You couldn't see it, but the stuffed bear made him smile. And although your daughter was not around when he passed, he was with her too, no matter the distance." Lorrena tried to stop speaking, but the words continued flowing through her mouth, regardless of how much sense they made.

"It may seem like he's gone, but he is always near you. Even in the cold winter air, he'll send you the scent of roses as beautiful as the ones you gave him after he passed away. And the most important thing of all, he's assuring you it wasn't your fault, Patricia. There was nothing you could have done to save him. You can't blame yourself." Lorrena blinked, looking at Patricia and her daughter, seeking some sort of approval. Suddenly, the force let her go. The tone of her voice lifted. "Am I right about all of this? Please tell me it means something."

Denise held onto the little girl's shoulders.

Patricia took in a deep breath before she spoke.

CHAPTER THIRTEEN

Patricia Pollaski

Friday -- February 27ᵗʰ -- 4:54 p.m.

"You looked up those names. There's no way you could have known about my friend, or my mother, or Jimmy for that matter," Patricia said, shaking her head. "There's just no way. This has to be a joke."

"I wouldn't joke about this," Lorrena said. "It hurt me to see your reaction earlier, but here I am, telling you again. I'm even hurting my mother's ears, talking about my visions. She says I'm crazy, but now I know this is no hallucination."

"Lorrena, I never said such a thing. I assured you that—"

"Leave it alone, Erin," Mrs. Gedolewen said. "It's Lorrena's turn to talk."

Lorrena did not respond to her mother. Instead she looked right at Patricia, her young eyes filled with a spark that burned deep within her pupils. "It's true, I'm not even seventeen years old yet. I can't imagine the pain you're going through after losing your son. But this message is his, not mine."

"This is insane. It's so absurd I don't know what else to say." Hot tears stung her eyes. She wanted to throw her arms up in the air, knock her head against the wall, but something inside of her resisted. The craze of her emotions subsided as the girl's predictions rang in her ears. Jimmy's arm moving as she held the stuffed bear above him. How else would she know if he wasn't here in the room? Patricia's sobs shook her body. Through the heaving sighs, she found the power to form words, though barely comprehensible. "He had so much time ahead of him, so many things to do. Why'd he have to leave me so soon?"

For a moment Lorrena was silent. A few of the residents had gathered in the back of the room to see what the commotion was, peeking through the dining room door. Others stood in the doorway leading to the hallway.

"It's a long story. A story I will tell you, just as Jimmy promised you the day he died," Lorrena said finally.

"He what?"

"A promise he made," Lorrena said. "But he needs my help."

"He promised me he would take care of himself. If I let him move from New England, he'd make the trip worthwhile. As a mother, you learn to trust your gut feeling," Patricia sucked in a couple of breaths to calm herself as her tears flowed faster. "I ignored it. Something in my heart wasn't right, but I let him go anyway. He would still be alive now if I'd kept him here, or if I'd convinced him not to get that motorcycle."

Lorrena lowered her head, staring intently at the ground. The lights in the room shone brighter. As she continued, the deep tone of her voice intensified once again. "But he's assuring you there's nothing you or anyone else could have done to prevent it. Life is like that. Things happen, and we can't go back to change them. The concept of time appears to move us forward. We must accept the way things are, learn from our experiences, and move on." She appeared to be in a trance, her focus isolated. "Now he wants you to use your gift of compassion to help people realize that life is far from over. Remind them to enjoy the beauty of the earth and to bask in the sheer joy of being alive in the moment. Let the love that exists within you shine. Listen to what the world has to say without letting your doubts overcome you. There is a story behind everything." Lorrena shut her eyes.

Dramatically, Lorrena's eyelids pulled apart, her chin lifting sharply. To Patricia's surprise, Mr. Anderson, Mrs. Leopold, even Mrs. Reynolds, followed Lorrena's gaze, the alertness in the residents' eyes reviving. Their mouths widened at the spectacle, which to Patricia remained invisible. Patients leaned on each other as they pointed, their canes falling to the floor.

A smile gleamed on Mrs. Gedolewen's face.

"What is it, Grammy P, what is it?" Anna asked. "What are they so excited about?"

Without answering, Patricia watched Denise crouch down behind Anna, locking her arms around her daughter's waist. Anna's hair stuck to her mother's cheek as she spoke in her ear. "Shh, Anna. Listen. Uncle Jimmy is talking to us."

"Oh yes, Uncle Jimmy," Anna said. "I know."

"There is only a bit more that he can share with you," Lorrena announced. "He wants you to know that his life's plan was a short one. In his heart, he always knew that, even when he was a boy. But he wants to assure you that part of him will live on. The way he's touched the world won't ever really disappear. This is when you must set your grief aside. Understand that there is no death, and no matter how much it hurts, you are alive. It is the ache, in fact, that assures it. The pain we associate with dying is merely the harsh realization that we will be okay, and that our only option is to keep going. If we recognize that our suffering won't continue forever, that life persists through physical deterioration, then there is potential to move through the grieving process, the outcome leaving us stronger."

Patricia couldn't believe her ears. How could the things coming out of this girl's mouth be real? A part of her felt as if she were still stuck in one of her awful dreams—dreams of Jimmy that felt so real until the reality of the morning emerged again, and her son disappeared. But there was no waking up from this moment, Patricia knew. The girl's words were as real as the tears falling from her eyes. As real as a mother and daughter reuniting after twenty years, beside a mother and daughter rejoicing at the end of the day. As genuine as the awareness in the residents' faces. No matter how it defied rationality, the evidence—however elusive—sat right there before her.

"I want to have faith in it," Patricia insisted. "I just—"

"I will write it out." Lorrena's voice had lost its slow, drawn-out quality. Her face was bright, her motions energetic. "Just like he promised. Then you will see that it's true."

Just as Patricia was about to open her mouth again, she stopped. She waited for Mrs. Marietta to weave through the residents to where she stood in the center of the lobby.

"What's all of the commotion in here?"

Patricia wiped her face with the sleeve of her scrubs. "The light you saw in your patient's room that time," Patricia said.

157

"Did you see something? Is that what this is about?"

"No, I didn't see anything," Patricia said. "I think—"

Lorrena's eyes lit up. Beside her, Erin mumbled under her breath.

"Just because you can't see a person, Erin, doesn't mean they're not there. It doesn't mean they're gone." Mrs. Gedolewen spoke firmly. "I'm not ever going to leave you, no matter if you want it that way or not. Don't you understand?" The old woman leaned forward in her wheelchair. Pushing one of her fragile elbows into the chair's handle, she attempted to lift herself to her feet. Patricia rushed over, Lorrena and Mrs. Marietta following closely behind.

"What are you doing, Mrs. Gedolewen? Sit down. Please don't hurt yourself. There's no need for you to stand," Patricia proclaimed, gently grabbing hold of the woman's arms to lower her back down into the seat.

"Yeah, Gram, you've already traveled too much today. Sit down," Lorrena said.

Patricia nodded as she ran her hands along Mrs. Gedolewen's sweater. "What you need to do is take off your wet clothes, so you don't get sick. Rest for a while."

"I'm not going anywhere until I can give my daughter a hug."

Erin hesitated before stepping slowly toward her mother, her heels clunking against the floor. Erin's face remained blank, her complexion pale aside from the red hue beneath her eyes. Patricia shuffled aside. As Erin leaned forward, Mrs. Gedolewen stood up to meet her. Watching them embrace, warmth radiated through Patricia's body, which gave way to a rush of shivers, raising the hairs on her arms.

"I'd understand if you didn't forgive me," Erin said into Mrs. Gedolewen's ear.

Mrs. Gedolewen pulled back gently, looking her daughter in the face. "Right after you ran away I swore that I wouldn't," she said, "but I couldn't remain angry forever. I thought we would always have the chance to reunite, although I'll admit I was beginning to lose hope. Time, whatever it is, has a way of screwing up your mind." Mrs. Gedolewen coughed, the sound rumbling deep in her lungs. "Your face appears so different now. Calmer, more mature. But in a way it's the same face that smiled up at me as I tucked the blanket beneath your chin at night. The same face that hid beneath the covers when I woke you up the next morning for school. Although it alters, it's the same face I've been losing and regaining for lifetimes."

"Listen to you. Besides your gray hair and your lack of mobility, you haven't changed either," Erin said. The ruthless glare on her face faded to a slight smile.

"Oh, but in many ways we have. More than we know. If you can finally accept your daughter and I for who we are, then we can move on from this part of our life, and allow the next chapter to begin."

Erin didn't move. "I guess we have no other option but to move forward."

Engulfed in their exchange, Patricia couldn't help but smile. When she felt a hand on her shoulder, her daze fell away. To her surprise, all of the residents who had surrounded her for what seemed like minutes ago were now gone, leaving only Anna and Lorrena in the corner. Denise stood by Patricia's side.

Patricia blinked to regain her bearings. The room had grown darker; the pounding of the rain against the roof had died down.

Denise circled her arms around Patricia's shoulders. "Mom, Anna is getting antsy. She's hungry. I think we're going to leave now."

"You are? What time is it?"

"Almost five, and the rain already changed to sleet. The weather advisory says to keep off the roads tonight, and all morning tomorrow."

"Already five? Are you serious? I should be on my way out now, too," Patricia said. "Let me finish up. I just have to find Mrs. Marietta and clock out. Follow behind me on the way to our house for dinner, yes? You can stay in your old bedroom so you don't have to drive home."

"Sure, Mom. We'd love to," Denise said.

"Mrs. Gedolewen—I mean, Miriam. How about I take you back to your room before I go?" Patricia asked. The woman sat upright in her wheelchair, her eyes focused into the distance. Erin stood a few feet away from her, their stares no longer converging.

"No, you take off. I'll make it back there somehow, don't you worry."

Erin's head perked up. "Well, I think we're heading out too. Okay, Lorrena? No more late-night strolls in the snow."

"No, Mom. I want to stay here. I don't want to leave Gram."

Mrs. Gedolewen coughed again. "As you wish, child. I'm sure no one will mind if you stay in the empty bed beside mine."

"Oh, could I?" Lorrena asked.

"I guess it's up to Patricia," Erin replied.

"Of course it's fine," Patricia called out from the office. She found Mrs. Marietta sitting behind the desk, her hands folded on top.

"You're leaving now, hmm? Please drive safe. I know you're close to home, but you know how unpredictable the roads can be in the winter," Mrs. Marietta said.

"I will. Thank you."

"Yes. I'm glad to see you're doing better."

Patricia put her time card into the machine until it clicked, the blue ink indicating it was already twenty minutes past her scheduled shift. "It's strange. In a matter of hours, I feel different."

Mrs. Marietta smiled, sliding her glasses higher onto her nose. Her bubbly eyes lit up as she waved.

Patricia left the office, signaling Denise toward the door. Anna jumped up and down, shouting, "Home, home! Anna's tummy is so, so hungry!"

"I know, Anna. You'll just have to wait."

Before they could make it outside, Mrs. Gedolewen called to them. "You know, I won't allow you to leave without a hug, Patricia. Who knows the next time you'll see me."

"Oh, don't worry, Miriam. I'll see you tomorrow. I'll be back for the evening shift," Patricia said. She gently wrapped her arms around the old woman's delicate body. Her ear brushed against the woman's soft, gray hair.

"Yes," Mrs. Gedolewen said. "Perhaps you will."

"Good bye, Miriam," Patricia said.

"Good bye, Patricia."

Before Patricia could utter a word, Lorrena had already begun pushing her grandmother back toward her room. Patricia looked around for Erin to follow them, but she was already gone.

"Stay close behind me in your car," Patricia said. She picked up her poncho from the chair, still wet from earlier, and threw it over her head. "In case anything happens, I can help you."

"Yes, Mom," Denise replied, "but I'm sure everything

will be fine."

Lifting Anna into her arms, Patricia pushed open the door with her hip to find a thick sheet of freezing rain pouring from the sky. The sound of the sleet resonated against the pavement. Patricia's sneakers sunk in the slushy mess as she darted down the walkway. Shielding Anna's head as best she could, the girl cried out. "It's cold, Grammy P!"

"I know, honey. We'll be home, warm and cozy beside the fire sooner than you can imagine." Patricia slid open the back door of her daughter's gray minivan, fastening Anna into her car seat. "See you soon," she said.

Patricia hurried to her car parked in the staff parking lot at the side of the building. The engine of her Volvo roared to life. Buckling her seatbelt, she listened to the hum of the engine as it warmed. The windshield wipers thrust back and forth. Taking off slowly down the road, she caught sight of her daughter's van behind her. Reaching to turn down the heat, she realized the arrow pointed at the cold.

Odd, she thought. She tried replaying the strange assortment of feelings, which had rushed through her body earlier, but the peculiar sensation of astonishment that life could appear out of the ordinary, was slowly slipping away. She found herself wanting to speak with Lorrena further. As her hands gripped the cold steering wheel, she was again left with only memories of her son, translucent and fleeting. The proof of her son's communication could never be held safe in her arms.

"If you can really hear me, Jimmy, give me a sign," Patricia said out loud. "Let me know you're here with me." Silence filled the air except for the sound of the tires pushing through the puddles. How was it possible to hear voices that weren't really spoken? Patricia sighed with frustration. She listened intently, but still there was no response.

As the road curved and straightened out, Patricia glanced in her rearview mirror. The night's thick haze obscured her from seeing any cars behind her. Out of impulse, she made a right turn down Harper Street, an alternative route to her home instead of continuing on the main road. Although she couldn't see her daughter's van, she hoped Denise had seen her make the turn.

There were fewer streetlights on this road, but the frequent houses let off their own illumination. On all sides, the streets were empty aside for a lone sand truck driving steadily by in the opposite lane, dumping a mix of salt and sand onto the road as the precipitation battered down harder.

Patricia approached the dead-end road leading to her driveway. As she pulled up to her house, the automatic light flickered on. Dashing from her car to the door, she found the inside of her house warm and welcoming. A fire roared in the fireplace, and the aroma of roasted garlic floated in the air.

"Jim?" she called out.

"Oh good, you're home," her husband said from the kitchen. "I made dinner for us. Did you have a good day at work?"

"I guess you could say that," Patricia said. "I'll tell you about it when we eat. I'm worried. Denise and Anna were supposed to be following me from the nursing home. I hope nothing bad happened."

"I'm sure they're okay," Jim said. Hustling over to the bin where they kept the mail, he pulled out a letter secured in a manila envelope. "Read this while you're waiting." Jim handed her the letter, postmarked from Arizona.

"Arizona? Who in the world is writing us from there?"

"Just read it."

Patricia carefully pulled out the letter, hand-written in

blue ink, and began to read:

To the Pollaskis,

It is difficult to know what to say. First, I will start with my name. I am Mark Humphrey. I am seventeen years old. Weeks ago I received information that a heart would be available for me from an unknown donor. Only a short time before that, the doctors had told me I may not live long enough to make a transplant. Already waiting in the hospital room to undergo bypass surgery, the heart was finally transported to my hospital, just in time. My body took to the new heart well and so recovery has been speedy since.

For many difficult years, I suffered from multiple congenital heart defects. At the age of fourteen, I was put on a list to find a new heart, and hopes were running low as the wait grew long. I missed much of my high school years. Because of your son's donation, I am able to finish my studies and eventually go to college. My dream is to become a doctor so I can help other people like me who are in need of new organs.

I wanted deeply to contact you to inform you of my graciousness. I begged my mother to find out about my donor and although it took much work to find you, I know that it was needed, for both of our families. I hope to someday meet you, to learn more about your son, since now he is a big part of me. I want you to know I am extremely grateful to your family. I thank you, in your son's honor, for this second chance at life.

Sincerely,
Mark

Patricia looked up from the letter, which was shaking in her hand. Tears streamed down her face. She wiped them away, a bittersweet smile ascending over her lips. "Well, I'll be damned. The girl was right."

Her husband eyed her with a puzzled look. "Patricia, what girl? It was a boy he saved. What are you talking about?"

"Nothing," Patricia said. "She'll explain it to you, soon. It was Jimmy's promise."

Jim's eyebrows rose. Shaking his head, he opened his arms to hug to her. Stepping toward him, Patricia rested her head on his shoulder, welcoming the warmth of his arms around her for the first time since their trip to the hospital, just after they'd learned their son would not survive. She could see only a broad blanket of darkness out of the window, and their image reflecting over it on the glass. Patricia raised her eyes. A pair of headlights cut their way through the black surface.

"They're home," Patricia said, breaking free from her husband's embrace. Hurrying to the door, she met her daughter and granddaughter, soaked with sleet.

"Gosh, I'm sorry I couldn't follow you, Mom. Anna was screaming and crying so loud for some food, and so I stopped quickly to pick up some crackers for her. Then we got held up because of an accident on Washington Street, just after Warner's Church. I was so scared that it might've been you. It happened right about the time we would have driven past."

"I didn't go that way," Patricia said. "I took Harper Street instead."

"Really? I thought you hated taking the back roads."

"Not tonight," Patricia said. A long pause followed. "You know, we have some good news, Denise. You need to read this." Grabbing the letter from the table, a coin hidden beneath it slid onto the floor with a soft clink. She was about to take a step forward, but instead she reached down to pick up the penny, which had fallen face up. She held the cold penny flat in her palm. The date was the same as the year Jimmy had been born. Patricia wiped her eyes.

"Is everything okay, Mom?"

"Yes, everything's fine." Patricia took in a deep breath, felt the vivacity of the air moving through her body. Her eyes lingered for a moment in the space between the window and the kitchen. "Now, let's go have dinner," she said, smiling. "Together. All of us."

CHAPTER
FOURTEEN

Lorrena Shaw

Friday -- February 27th -- 5:24 p.m.

L orrena nearly burst into a jog as they approached her
grandmother's room.

"Slow down, child," Mrs. Gedolewen said. "I
feel like we're on an amusement ride. Why suddenly in such a
rush?"

Holding her hands against her forehead, Lorrena winced.
"It's all so clear right now," she said. "This has never happened before. It's so strange. It's like I can see bits of Patricia's life piercing through my head, overpowering me. I have
to write it in my journal. You said to write it down. I don't
want to forget it." As she heaved open the door, Lorrena
wheeled her grandmother over to the bedside, abandoning her
to retrieve the notebook and pen from her backpack. She started to scribble down the events that had taken place in the lob-

by, and at the beach.

A cough echoed through her grandmother's lungs. "Whoa now, one step at a time. There shouldn't be any hurry. The Records are always available, as long as your mind is free from thought. How else did you know what to say to that woman? Those words certainly weren't coming from you."

Lorrena looked up into her grandmother's face. Squinting through her glasses, her grandmother's eyes appeared weary and worn out. The lines drawn across her skin seemed to have multiplied.

"But what if I can't put everything down to paper? How will I write the story?"

"Have I not taught you anything?" Her grandmother's face remained blank.

"You've taught me more than I can even comprehend," Lorrena said. She thought back to the night at the dinner table when she first learned of her grandmother's existence. So much had happened since then, it felt like a lifetime ago.

"Patience. There's no need for concern. I assure you that you don't even have to think, and it will come. That is the most thorough way to access your Records. As you travel out of your body or when you're meditating, mindless and free."

"But I think I know how it's going to end," Lorrena said, slamming her hands down on the bed. In the back of her mind, she could make out the fuzzy image of Patricia speaking to a man beside a desk. She wondered if the vision was happening that very second.

"Oh, Lorrena, Lorrena," her grandmother said. "If there's anything I must get through your head while I have the chance, it's that there are no ends. Don't you see? The endings are only illusions. They're not real."

Lorrena dropped her pen and her notebook onto the chair.

"How will I manage to write that in my book? It has to end somewhere, doesn't it? If it goes on forever there'll be too many pages, and no one will ever want to read it."

"What I'm saying is that just because a story runs out of pages, doesn't mean it's over. Your book will certainly have to stop somewhere. But everything starts and ends in moments that are always preceded by something else, always contained within a larger context. Eternity—have you heard—" Her words were cut off by another fit of coughing.

Lorrena leapt to her grandmother's side. "Gram, are you okay?"

Mrs. Gedolewen's eyes closed, her hand covering her mouth. "I just need you to help me take off this sweater. I need to rinse my face and rest."

"Sure," Lorrena said as her cell phone buzzed in her pocket. She pulled it out to reveal a message from Ariel. *For sale sign is taken down. Are you coming back soon? I miss your ghost stories.*

Lorrena texted back: *Many stories to tell, you won't even believe. Business to clear up with Edna too. Soon.*

Tossing her phone into her bag, she peeled the damp cardigan sweater from her grandmother's arms. Under it, she found a long-sleeve cotton shirt, also touched with moisture. Lorrena rolled up the sleeves to feel her grandmother's arms.

"Gram, you're freezing. Why didn't you tell us earlier that your clothes were this bad?"

"There was no need to."

"But you don't want to catch pneumonia!"

"Reach into the dresser there, the second drawer from the top," her grandmother said. "You will find a white silk shirt and cotton pink skirt, the most comfortable clothes I own. I used to wear them when your grandfather took me out dancing. He would twirl me and spin me in circles until I was dizzy, my skirt flowing out like an enormous umbrella. I wish you could have seen us then."

"I wish." Lorrena pushed clothes aside, and found the outfit together at the bottom of the drawer, the shirt folded inside the flowing fabric of the skirt. Laying the clothes out on the bottom of the bed, she fixed the creases in the silk shirt. Next she attempted to smooth out the crinkled nature of the skirt, but as she ran her hand over it, the waves in the cloth returned.

"It's not like that because of the many years it's been folded, Lorrena," Mrs. Gedolewen said. "It's supposed to be like that."

"Oh, well it's beautiful all the same."

"Will you fetch a wash cloth from the bin inside the bathroom, and wet it with warm water?" her grandmother asked.

"Sure thing." As Lorrena spun the faucet handle and held her hand under it, she waited, watching herself in the mirror until the water slowly heated up. Scenes from the past few days surfaced, yet she saw them as if she were watching herself from beyond. The first time she saw her grandmother's house flashed before her eyes. The police car's blue and red lights as she walked back from the nursing home. Chasing after her dog as she bolted into the dark, snowy graveyard. How the wind swept the snow from the tree, landing on James' grave. She saw herself leaving her teacher and the school behind as she hustled toward her grandmother's room. The moment she first met her grandmother, smiling back at her from her bed. And she saw the shock on Patricia's face when she confessed James' presence. When Lorrena got the chance, she would write it all down.

"Ouch," she said, pulling her hand back as the water began to steam. Soaking the cloth, she folded it into a neat square.

"I'm going to need some help," her grandmother said. Her voice was barely audible from around the corner.

"I'm coming." Lorrena spun around in the doorway. She laid the cloth on one handle of the wheelchair. "First, we'll dress you in the most elegant of threads," Lorrena said, raising her chin up as if speaking to royalty.

"But of course," her grandmother said. She lifted her arms wearily, not even to a vertical position as Lorrena slid off the cotton shirt to replace it with the dazzling silk one. Her grandmother winced as her hands drifted down against her thighs. Lorrena struggled to pull the skirt up her grandmother's thin legs, until finally, she couldn't help but smile at the sight before her. An old woman all dressed up to rest.

"You look like you are going to the ball of your dreams," Lorrena said.

"Maybe that idea is not too far off." Mrs. Gedolewen smiled.

At that comment, Lorrena's entire being became engulfed in sadness. "I would love to escort you there. That way I can watch you dance, just like you said."

"Perhaps you will, and only then, we will dance together until the morning light pulls at your eyelids." Her grandmother shook a finger toward Lorrena, her words ringing in a playful tune.

Lorrena lowered her head without answering.

"Come now, don't be sad, child. There's no time for it. I still need to get out of this seat."

Lorrena raised her eyes slowly. She held out her hand for her grandmother, but as the old woman moved to stand up, her legs collapsed beneath her and she fell back into the chair.

"Ah, see? My body is finally beginning to fail me."

"You're fine. You just need to rest," Lorrena encouraged.

Lorrena wrapped her arm around her grandmother, lifting her up and onto the mattress. She fluffed the pillows, guiding them under her grandmother's back. Setting the back of her hand against her grandmother's cheek, Lorrena found her skin to be cold. She took the warm cloth from the chair and gently pressed it against her grandmother's face.

"Much better. I am so glad it is you here to help me. It is the greatest gift, you know, to have you beside me," her grandmother said, holding her hand up toward Lorrena's face before closing her eyes. She carefully folded her hands together in her lap.

"It is. I want you to tell me again, the story about how you knew I was coming here before I did."

"That story is an old one, my dear. Sit down and I'll tell you one that I don't know."

Still holding onto her grandmother's hand, Lorrena plopped down into the green chair beside the bed, resting her head against the mattress. "Don't you mean one that *I* don't know? How can you tell me a story if you don't know it yourself? I thought you knew everything."

"I was young and naïve like you once. No matter our age, there are some things even the greatest of clairvoyants can't tell, for there must always be some secret to life to make it entirely worth living," her grandmother said. "The books of our lives are best when we get so caught up in the all-encompassing world of our story that each moment we burn with anticipation. We deeply crave what will happen next, or maybe we don't care at all. Maybe we're depressed and we just want it all to end because we simply cannot go on any longer. But we stick it out. We have to. Because sometimes we can't avoid conflict in the story of our lives. It's the driving force. More often than not, we face it head on."

"Ouch," Lorrena mumbled.

"Ouch is right. Sometimes life hurts. Like my body, my hip, my voice. They hurt. But what about the other times? When we're bored, and maybe we wish we had a good fight to keep us busy. Then we find that we're waiting. Always waiting for something we can't quite put our finger on. Something, anything to happen. Waiting to know how it all will end." Her grandmother coughed and then went silent.

"Well?"

"Well what?" Her grandmother's eyes remained shut. "Oh, you don't feel as though my story has finished?"

"No, no, keep going. There's more. I still don't understand yet, how you don't know what's going to happen next?"

"Oh, okay. Where was I again? Oh yes. The end. You know how when a good book ends, you're ripped from the certainty of its pages, returned to the harsh actuality of the unknown? The world of the story crumbles around you because you've finally reached that final page, the page you were dying to arrive at, and now you're there. It's done. You wish you could go back and read it again, but in essence you must keep going. Onward, to the next story. To stories within the ultimate Universal story of absolute Love that ties each and every single person of the world who has ever lived, together. Just as mine is tied to yours, it breaks away. The loss of life can be like that too, as we constantly remain in anticipation of our purpose. The theme of the whole of our life. What was the point? Did I do everything I came here to do? Can I leave these people, knowing it will take the illusion of their end to reunite with me? To leave them, their thoughts lingering toward..."

Her grandmother paused. Lorrena was unsure if she

would continue speaking. Still, she waited, watching her grandmother's eyelids pulsing as they remained closed. Finally, the old woman blew a puff of air outward, her words floating through it.

"That is the hardest part. When we are seemingly forced to think too far ahead to the parts we can't envision. We reach a roadblock when we try to imagine this so-called conclusion. When we push to that point, we become gloomy again. Because after trying to piece together all the way up to that instant where everything we could possibly think about our lives has already been said and done, where is there to go? Our minds are forced to stop thinking because end is end, is end. Wedged within time, we simply cannot fathom it."

"But you just said there were no ends, Gram. Why do you have to confuse me?"

Mrs. Gedolewen's eyebrows turned in, though her eyes remained closed. Abruptly, her voice was plagued with unease. "Erin, you're not listening. If you listened, you would know without any doubt. Even as the wind blows its final storm through our lungs, after our heart pumps its final push of blood and the waves of the brain eliminate the thoughts that plague us, it may be the end of this body, but the soul, it burns with new life! Do you understand, Erin? You never listen. Stop yelling at me and listen!"

"But I'm not—"

"Do you remember? A few years ago, I told you the time that you came to me crying as I sat in the garden watering the perennials, covered from head to toe in dirt. You were afraid of the Death Monster, and I told you he was not a big, dark monster to be scared of, but a being of light. Nothing to fear, Erin, do you recall?"

"Gram, it's me. Lorrena. We're in the nursing home, and

you just put on your dancing clothes, and you're telling me the story you didn't know."

"Lorrena? You are—" Her grandmother's face twitched. "Oh…yes. I'm so sorry. I must stop speaking aloud. Everything is flashing before me, out of order now, I see—"

"Are you okay? What do you see?"

"Ed. Sit down, Ed. My feet aren't able to hold me up yet. I can't dance, no not yet."

"Gram, are you okay? It's Lorrena here."

"Yes. Lorrena. I have never felt better, although I'm holding on, a bit. I feel your hand, child. Do not worry. I know you don't want me to let—"

A tear trickled down Lorrena's cheek. Gently squeezing her grandmother's hand, she watched the old woman's face smooth out. Laying her head down against the edge of her grandmother's pillow, she wished she could freeze this moment in time. Sit beside her grandmother forever, listening to the stories she told so firmly in her profound, melodic voice. Their time together had been so short. *If only I had come earlier. No. That wasn't how things were supposed to go.*

"It's all right then," Lorrena said. "You don't have to."

"Let me tell you. Even a minute ago, I did not know what it felt like. I didn't know, and still I do not, but I will, soon," her grandmother said. Lorrena took in entirely, the distinct sound of her grandmother's words, growing softer, raspier. "For me, the illusion of this story subsides. For you, you must keep going. Value every moment, every word there is to write."

"I will," Lorrena said. "Are you sure you're okay?"

"Yes. Never more at peace. Can I rest my voice now?"

"Yes. Can I rest beside you?"

"Always."

175

As Lorrena shut her eyes, the image of the nursing home shifted into bright colors. A part of Lorrena's consciousness urged her to question. What would come next, what would tomorrow bring?

Lorrena mumbled out loud, "Now I will push the thoughts away, listen to the sound of the particles bouncing off each other in the air."

She heard the faint hiss of her grandmother's breathing, the hum of the radiator, the bustle of a few people walking through the corridor, until finally her thoughts disintegrated. As she let go, she again heard a voice, separate from her mind, speaking to her from outside.

Lorrena listened as James' voice grew stronger in the distance.

EPILOGUE

"All goes onward and outward, nothing collapses,
And to die is different from what anyone supposed, and luckier."
— Walt Whitman

Jimmy Pollaski

Every day of my life I lived to prove death's delusion. The years transformed me from child to teenager, and before I knew it, I entered the beginning and the end of my adulthood. Many times within the silent rotation of the calendar, even in my younger years, I was infested with constant curiosity. What would it feel like to die? How would I know when it happened? Within the core of my bones, I felt that my time on Earth would be brief—that my life would cease before I proceeded into all that I blindly prepared for. As children are often asked what they want to be when they grow up, my dreams would only take me as far as the word's definition assumes. I wanted to open my own restaurant on the water, serving the finest foods and a view of ocean's expanse—the expanse of my dreams evaporated.

In the back of my mind, I was constantly reminded of a place not too far away, which would claim me in a manner I could not then imagine. Yet, no matter how I ended up passing over, like everyone else I would not be alive to tell about it. I would never be able to dictate the release of the Self from the body, the serene sensation of slipping from the weight of physical form.

Or would I? Could I find a way to share with the whole of humankind that death was nothing to fear? That it was all merely a segment of the ever-spinning cycle of life, not just as the seasons changed the world's costumes, but as our own were shed? Our Divine Selves, finding new temporary outfits to try on, and return—rebirth, death, and again. A process we had all gone through before as the earth continued to spin. Could I relay it to remind them all even when their embodied attire sheltered the answers?

Yes, it was a promise I had made. Etched within the invisible book describing the paths of our lives, under our control only to a certain degree, our free will taking the backseat to the certain events we cannot avoid.

It was my time.

During the last few days of my life, I felt this fleetingness of time as it moved through my fingers. Something indistinct in the air reminded me of the magnitude of every second—how the present so easily slipped away into the past, lost, and there was nothing we could do but let it pass into preceding moments.

I tightened my grip on the handlebars of my motorcycle while the wind, uncontainable, pressed against my face, sent my hair in different directions, pushed around the palm trees towering above me as the waves grew and collapsed over the ocean. The ground beneath me was solid; the dotted lines on the road passed under my wheels, but the path ahead of me remained unclear. The fog early that morning, the morning I would later drive my motorcycle into the side of a cliff, consumed the area, slowly evaporating as the sun climbed higher in the sky. Yes, it was only a matter of time before the days aligned, my path leading me here. The motorcycle's engine roaring beneath me, the earth and the ocean smearing together at seventy miles per hour. Attending school that morning for a meeting with my advisor to determine my classes for the following semester. Paths of everyone on Earth intersecting, and diverging, and intersecting. The truck shipping produce to a nearby grocery store had hit traffic on its way from Los Angeles. The driver who was supposed to be making the run had taken the day off sick, the driver's substitute on his first big trip in the truck.

I awakened to my alarm buzzing in my ears, the cool breeze pushing my curtains up to the world gone gray beyond the windows. Throwing on my clothes, my motorcycle waited outside. I hopped aboard, flying down the hill leading to the freeway. Prepared for the exhilaration of the freeway's roundabout entrance, which led to the lanes where I'd typically fly freely through cars, blood pumping through my veins. Fast approaching, the green arrow lit up, signaling—paths preparing to intersect. I bore left. And—

I can't say it all happens in slow motion. It's drawn out, yet swift as if time has no meaning, no substance. In a blur of air, the truck veers off to the left, over the lines that have yet to pass under me. Directly into the path of the left turn I'm taking, where I make it just short of the freeway entrance. My tight grip on the motorcycle. The truck's horn piercing through the air. I'm flying toward the cliff that stands tall above the road. The truck has fallen across the opposite breakdown lane. I'm lying on my back, looking up into the blinding light of the sun, shining hard on my face. Nourishment to the wounds running down the front of my body, bleeding out no pain. Faces looking down at me. *I'm okay*, I'm saying. *Okay*. The voices are shrill, unresponsive to my responses. I tell them I'm okay. We're losing him, I hear them yell, the sounds drawing outward, growing distant. I try to move my hands, shake my head, '*No*.' Blue and red lights flash into the white light as it engulfs me, the silver cord extending upward from my stomach, pulling me.

With a snap that I don't hear, the cord severs. I'm floating—over the road, the cliff, the hospital. All at once, the delicate hand of my grandmother transfers its warmth through my body like a comet grazing the sky with a sudden, hot glow. She's been waiting for me. The beeping in the hospital room echoes in my ears. I hear voices singing magnificent melodies from beyond, soothing, so happy to welcome me back, except...

My mother's sobs ring off in the distance. Her hands fold together as she collapses into the chair beside my dad, his arm cradling her descent. Her face contorts. Tossing her head into her hands, I tell her what I want her to know. *I'm okay*.

"My story isn't over, Mom," I say, my words suspended. The scenes close in around me, a tunnel of astounding radiance forming. Shards of illumination multiply without hurting my eyes. "I promise, I will tell you the true story. Our story."

The experiences leading us to this moment. My accident and beyond—no, can I change that word? There are no accidents, no mistakes. I chose this. My parents. My birthplace and my death—my own precious plan of growth. My Divine Self, constantly expanding.

I am dying today, but the world around me fades to light. The silent pull of the world's forces beckon us, urging us to remember the purpose of gaining strength, first by losing it. Had I encountered all I had come here to experience this time around? To recall life's essence beyond ourselves? To remember death's grief, and its hope—blind to many of the human eye to keep us hurting, but going nevertheless—a cycle. As our stories approach their ends, the illusion subsides, even when the words trail off, when the heart ceases to beat, our voices silenced.

I raise my voice to remind you. The pain is not forever, no—listen, the voices inaudible yet present, eternal—forever our guidance, and whispering.

AFTERWORD

I t's hard to pinpoint exactly where stories come from. Imagination and inspiration often merge with bits and pieces of our real lives, and then require lots of research. Stories come from everywhere.

Just before finishing my last year as an English major at Rhode Island College in Providence, the idea for this novel was born on one fateful summer day when my car collided with another. It was only a minor accident, the first one in my life, but I will never forget the awful sound of cars colliding, the fear that surged through my body. I tried hard not to bash myself for being an awful driver. The busy four-lane highway with one little turning lane in its center and no traffic lights begged for such an incident. I replayed the accident in my head, my left-hand turn into.... *Boom*. It was as if the black SUV had fallen out of the sky, right in front of me. If only I had not agreed to substitute my co-worker's gymnastics class that day, on her birthday, this never would have happened. If only I could go back and do the turn again, safely. If only...

I pulled over, met the man in the other car while we waited for the police to arrive. Turned out, he was in a rental car visiting Rhode Island all the way from southern California.

"I'm going to move there someday," I blurted out, though the homebody side of me that had spent its entire existence on the east coast did not truly believe it.

As we spoke about the California freeways and his insistence that there was nothing out west as dangerous as these

Rhode Island roads, my mind drifted.

There are no accidents, I thought. *Maybe I have to write about this.*

When I returned home that day, in search of some sort of consolation, I found none. In fact, it got worse. It was also on this day that a friend lost his childhood friend in a motorcycle accident out in California, an hour away from the hometown of the guy I had just met. Though I did not know him, I was devastated for my friend and for the young man's family.

A month passed. Autumn hit, and I began my search for higher education in creative writing. Rhode Island was nice, but California continued to call my name, a faint whisper in my heart. As a kid, just like I knew I wanted to be a writer and that I could not live without gymnastics, I also knew that eventually I would find myself living in a place with constant summer-like seasons, no matter how scared I was of leaving home. When I found the M.F.A. program at Chapman University in Orange, CA, I knew within the core of my being that I would end up there. My mother, however, protested. She insisted it was too far away, even though she really had no say— I was no longer her little girl, although, somewhere inside existed that same girl who had attempted story after story until she realized she did not know enough about life to write a real novel.

I had written many short stories, and felt I might be onto something. As the events in my life continued to subtly lead me where I needed to go, I realized that these very events were summoning the story I needed to write. Not just my story, but other peoples' stories, together: my first character was a young man at the peak of his potential who died suddenly, but still had a message for those he had left behind on Earth. All he needed to do was to find a medium to communicate. I held the ideas in the back of my mind, unsure of when I would attempt this first novel.

Soon after I applied to Chapman, I got word of a young woman who would be transferring to our school to compete on our gymnastics team. Her family lived just 20 minutes away from my prospective school. Her mother offered for me to stay at their house, and a few months later I left to visit California. Just like that, it was happening.

I feared being homeless and alone, three thousand miles from my family, but the scary parts continued to fill themselves in. During my visit, I was offered a part-time coaching job at my friend's gym. I met another friend from the gym, and we all went to a party on St. Patrick's Day, where I was introduced to more great people. I found my own place to live using a random website. After I packed up my bags and drove west, I learned that many of the people I met were connected. One roommate had gone to grade school with a friend from graduate school, and another roommate knew my co-worker. In fact, I had met my roommate's friends at the St. Patrick's Day party months before I had met her. I even found myself at the same party several years in a row after that. It was each of these coincidences that reminded me I was exactly where I was supposed to be. I realized that my novel must also show how people's life stories, seemingly separate, intertwined for a purpose.

Chapman required us to write a novel or collection of short stories for our graduate thesis, so I took the leap and began the first chapters, unsure exactly where they would lead me. While I knew Patricia's story would connect to Lorrena's in order to reach her son, I found myself writing to learn what would happen next. And like life, I realized events I had written were subconsciously leading me in the direction I needed to go to bring everyone together.

Over the past 15 years, I have also been guided toward many texts which helped me gain a better understanding of the world beyond the one we experience in our everyday physical reality—accounts of near-death experiences, memories of life between lives, out-of-body experiences—concepts that seem unbelievable. I have included the names of these books on the following page.

So, wherever it is our stories come from, do not be afraid to write and live out yours with all of your heart. Trust that our stories go on, always and forever.

Dear Reader,

Thank you so much for reading and supporting my work. If you enjoyed *Illusion of an Ending*, please take a second to leave me a review on Amazon or Goodreads, and visit me on your favorite social media site. Your support in helping to spread the word about this book means so much to me, especially as a new author and lifelong dreamer!

With love and gratitude,

Danielle Soucy Mills

DanielleSoucyMills.com

facebook.com/AuthorDanielleSoucyMills

twitter.com/DSoucyMills

instagram.com/DanielleSoucyMills

goodreads.com/DSoucyMills

SUPPLEMENTAL READING

Journey of Souls: Case Studies of Life Between Lives by Michael Newton, PhD

Through Time into Healing: How Past Life Regression Therapy Can Heal Mind, Body and Soul by Brian Weiss

Growing up in Heaven: The Eternal Connection Between Parent and Child by James Van Praagh

After Life: Answers from the Other Side by John Edward

Life on the Other Side: A Psychic's Tour of the Afterlife by Sylvia Browne

Home with God: In a Life the Never Ends by Neale Donald Walsch

Life After Death: The Burden of Proof by Deepak Chopra

Edgar Cayce on the Akashic Records by Kevin J. Todeschi

How to Read the Akashic Records: Accessing the Archive of the Soul and it's Journey by Linda Howe

Way of the Peaceful Warrior: A Book that Changes Lives by Dan Millman

Jonathan Livingston Seagull by Richard Bach

Astral Dynamics: The Complete Book of Out-of-Body Experiences by Robert Bruce

The Afterlife of Billy Fingers: How My Bad-Boy Brother Proved to Me There's Life After Death by Annie Kagan

Your Soul's Plan: Discovering the Real Meaning of the Life You Planned Before You Were Born by Robert Schwartz

ACKNOWLEDGEMENTS

I am eternally grateful for every person who has guided me along my path to write, publish, and promote this novel. First and foremost, thank you to my mother, Kathy, for being the most wonderful mom a girl could ask for and for sharing your passion of books with me since childhood. To my dad, Joel, my sister, Renee, and to my family on all sides. Your tremendous love and support has given me the courage to follow my dreams. A resounding thank you to my husband, Jesse. It sounds so trite, but I would not be *here* in this wonderful moment without you.

Thank you to the many teachers over the years that have encouraged me to expand my love for the written word. To Elizabeth, the reason I handwrote my first "novel" in a blue binder at a Montessori table. To Dr. K. for helping me get over my fear of writing for publication. To my professors at Rhode Island College, Dr. Karen Boren and Thomas Cobb, for helping me to hone my craft, and to explore options beyond a bachelor's degree.

A huge heartfelt thank you to my fellow Chapman MFA alums: Ali, Jonelle, Ryan, Jen, Natasha, Dave, Shannon, Ben, Nidzara, Penelope, Adam, Sarah, Pat, Jazmine, Courtney, Jill, Daniel, James, Cruz, Peter, and Mark, for your tough love in writing workshop. To my incredible professors: Dr. Martin Nakell, Jim Blaylock, Tim Powers, Dr. Mark Axelrod, and Alicia Kozameh, for your help in really making this book writing thing happen. Thanks to you, it is no longer just a goal, but a reality.

Thank you to my amazing beta readers and friends. To Stacey, Amy, Amanda, Ashley, Katie, Nicole, Jen, Gail, Maureen, Josie, Jill, Kim, Amber, Toni, Mike, Tanya, Marisa, Tarin, Corinne, Chris, Michelle, Akua, Heather, Ayumi, Taylor, and Scott. To Matt, for being my first whole book test subject. To Maria, who took a chance on my story on a whim and has believed in my abilities ever since. To Amy Lynne, for everything. You are my superhero. To Betty, for the beautiful cover picture, and of course, to Michael, for knowing we needed it in advance. To my indie author group: Danielle, Christine, Laura, Jill, Yvette, Chari, Kate, Gretchen, and Raquel, for all of your invaluable writing, publishing, and promoting advice and support. To Kim and Josh Soderberg, for your guidance in all things illustration and graphic design, including the Aerial Awareness logo. To Sheri, John, and Necole—beautiful souls who came into my life at just the right time.

Enormous gratitude for my wonderful editor, Michelle Josette. Thank you for your dedication to helping put the finishing touches on a book that has been eight years in the making. Your work has been invaluable to me. To Regina Wamba of Mae I Design, for my beautiful book cover and your hard work to truly capture my vision. To Chris Wood of SD Photo studio, for my author photo. And to Julie Titus of JT Formatting for formatting and interior design.

So much appreciation for everyone who has supported me and my work.

With every book we read, every person we meet, every event that takes place, no matter how big or small, good or bad, our lives are altered, changed, created. No matter its context. Thank you.

Made in the USA
San Bernardino, CA
18 December 2014